PUT A LID ON IT

# DONALD E. WESTLAKE

## PUT A LID ON IT

PRESS

Published by Warner Books

An AOL Time Warner Company

Mysterious Press books are published by Warner Books, Inc., 1271 Avenue of the Americas, New York, NY 10020.

Visit our Web site at www.twbookmark.com.

 An AOL Time Warner Company

The Mysterious Press name and logo are registered trademarks of Warner Books, Inc.
Printed in the United States of America
First Printing: April 2002

10  9  8  7  6  5  4  3  2  1

Library of Congress Cataloging-in-Publication Data

Westlake, Donald E.
   Put a lid on it / Donald E. Westlake.
      p. cm.
   ISBN 0-89296-718-8
      1. Presidents—Election—Fiction. 2. Political campaigns—Fiction. 3. Burglary—Fiction.
   I. Title.

PS3573.E9 P88 2002
813'.54—dc21                                          2001051435

My old friend Mickey Schwerner, who was murdered with James Chaney and Andy Goodman on a berm in Mississippi the night of June 21, 1964, by a group of political cretins, once in conversation described the American two-party system to me in these words, with which I have never found reason to argue: "It's the same old story," he said. "The moochers versus the misers."

This is for Mickey. Forest green.

PUT A LID ON IT

# 1

THE ELEVENTH DAY Meehan was in the MCC, the barbers came around to 9 South; two barbers, a white one for the white inmates, a black one for the rest. Each dragged a chair behind himself, with a guard following, and they set up in opposite triangles of the communal room, which was shaped like a six-pointed star, the cells outside that, in two facing lines in sword hilts sunk into five of the star's crotches: the exit to the concrete room where the elevators came was at the sixth.

So that was another difference from state or county jugs; no separate room for the barbers to ply their trade. After eleven days, Meehan was thinking he might write a monograph on the subject, was already writing it in his head. Never put anything on paper in stir: that was one of the ten thousand rules.

Of course, the primary difference between the Manhattan Correctional Center, which was where bail-less federal prisoners in the borough of Manhattan, city and state of New York, waited before and during their trials, was the attitude of the guards. The guards thought the prisoners were animals, of course, as usual, and treated them as such. But in this place the guards thought they themselves were not animals; that was the difference.

You get into a state pen, any state pen in the country—well, any state Meehan had been a guest in, and he felt he could extrapolate—and there was a real sense of everybody being stinking fetid swine shoveled into this shithole together, inmates and staff alike. There was something, Meehan realized, now that he was missing it, strangely comforting about that, about guards who, with every breath they took, with every ooze from their pores, said, "You're a piece of shit and so am I, so you got no reason to expect anything but the worst from me if you irritate my ass." These guards here, in the MCC, they buttoned all their shirt buttons. What were they, fucking Mormons?

Meehan had never been held on a federal charge before, and he didn't like it. He didn't like how inhuman the feds were, how unemotional, how you could never get around the Book to the man. Never get around the Book. They were like a place where the speed limit's 55, and they enforce 55. Everybody *knows* you enforce 70.

Shit. From now on, Meehan promised himself, no more federal crimes.

And this one was a wuss, this one was so lame. Him and three guys, whose names he would no longer remember, had a little hijack thing, off a truckstop, Interstate 84, upstate fifty miles north of the city, there was *no way* to know that truck held registered mail. Not a post office truck, a private carrier, no special notices on it at all. The truck Meehan and his former allies wanted, from the same carrier, was full of computer shit from Mexico. Meehan wasn't looking forward to making that plea to some jury.

But in the meantime, for who knows how long, here he was in the MCC, downtown Manhattan, convenient to the federal courts, thinking about his monograph on the differences between federal and non-federal pounds.

There were a number of ragheads on 9 South, Meehan presumed either terrorists with bombs or assholes who strangled their sisters for fucking around, and they all lined up to get their hair cut by the white barber. Johnson, a white inmate who'd been friendly and palsy with Meehan since he got here and who Meehan took it for granted was a plant, came over to help him watch the barbering, the two of them seated at one of the plastic tables in the middle of the communal room. "Every time," Johnson said, "those guys are first in line, get their hairs cut, never does any good."

Meehan, polite, said, "Oh?"

"Their hair grows too fast," Johnson told him. "It's something about the sand or something, where there's no water, you look at these guys, haircut haircut, end of the day they're back the way they were, they still look like a Chia toy."

"Chia toys take water," Meehan said.

"And sparrows take shit," Johnson said.

What was that supposed to mean? Meehan watched the piles of curly black oily hair mount up around the raghead in the chair, like they were gonna finish with a Joan of Arc here, and it occurred to him to wonder, as it had never occurred to him to wonder in a state pen, how come barbers were such a total criminal class. Everywhere you went, the barbers were inmates who happened on the outside to be barbers, so this was how they made bad money and good time on the inside, but the question was, how come so many barbers were felons? And what kind of *federal* crime can a barber pull? Maybe what happened, every jail around, whenever a barber was gonna finish his time, the word went out to the police forces of the world, keep your eyes on the barbers, we need one May 15. Could be.

A guard came into the block. His tan uniform was so neat,

he looked like he thought he was in the Pentagon. Maybe he really was in the Pentagon; who knew?

The guard came over to Meehan: "Lawyer visit."

That was a bit of a surprise. There wasn't much Meehan and his lawyer had to say to one another. But any distraction was welcome; rising, Meehan said, "I'm with you."

Johnson, friendly and genial, said, "Expecting good news?"

"Maybe I'm being adopted," Meehan said.

Turned out, he was.

# 2

THE FIRST THING Meehan noticed, the guy wasn't his lawyer. His court-appointed lawyer was a frizzy-haired skinny Jewish woman, maybe forty, dressed in that hairy crap they do, might as well be a chador, big golden hoop earrings for that feminine touch. And the second thing he noticed, the guy wasn't a lawyer at all.

But this was the place where the felons met up with their mouthpieces, down here on 4, a honeycomb of cubicles of leaded glass embedded with chicken wire, all the doors and door frames black metal, desks and chairs black metal, everything metallic and tight, everything you touched made a sound like the guillotine. Nice place.

"Come on in, Meehan," said his non-lawyer, gesturing from where he sprawled at the small metal table in the small glass room. A tan manila folder in front of him on the table provided a wan touch of color.

The guard stood behind Meehan, there was nowhere else he planned to go, so he shrugged and went to sit in the metal chair opposite the ringer, not bothering to read the tab on the folder, while the guard shut the door and went away, to give them as much privacy as you ever get in a place like this, which is none.

The ringer said, "How you doin, Meehan?"

Meehan lifted his right hand. First he did a come-to-me beckoning gesture, first finger, right hand, then he did a writing-on-a-pad gesture, then he put that hand palm down on the cool metal surface of the table.

The ringer was quick; at least there was that much. He reached into his gray-green checked sports jacket and came out with a small lined notepad and a retractable pen. He put both on the table near Meehan's hand, and Meehan opened the pad, past several pages of tiny unreadable black-ink notes, found a blank page, and wrote on it, "You're not a lawyer." Then he turned the pad so the guy could read it.

Which he did, scanned it quickly, nodded, shrugged, and said, "Ms. Goldfarb was reassigned to—"

Meehan held up his hand. When the guy stopped, Meehan slid the pad back, underlined the *a*, faced it around to the guy again: "You're not *a* lawyer."

This time, the guy actually studied what Meehan had written, then gave him a look that was curious, nothing more. He said, "Why do you say that?"

Meehan shook his head. He wasn't going to get along with this guy. "I didn't say it," he pointed out, "I wrote it."

"All right," the guy said, "why did you write it?"

"Because you don't say things in here." That was another of the ten thousand rules.

"Well, you've started," the guy said, "so go ahead. Why do you believe I'm not a lawyer?"

Meehan thought it over, and decided: what the hell. He said, "There's two kinds of— What do I call you?"

The guy seemed surprised. He said, "Jeffords."

"Okay, Mr. Jeffords. There's two kinds of lawyers come in here, boy lawyers and girl lawyers. The boy lawyers know they're representing scum, and they want to be thought of as something better than that, so they dress over the top, like a really successful Moscow pimp. Two-thousand-dollar suits, four-thousand-dollar watches, gold rings, Italian shoes the Pope couldn't afford. They don't get haircuts, they get coiffed, and they want you to know it." This was another monograph he'd done in his head. Continuing from it, he said, "Girl lawyers got a different situation. They can't come on like sexual beings, not in a place like this, so they go for the dikes-on-a-camping-trip look, your baggy wool slacks, bulky Irish-knit sweaters, Beatles haircut. None of them, boys or girls, dress like you, like you're going to a neighbor's barbeque. And none of them sprawl, like you're doing, they all sit up straight, because they're at work. The guy on this side of the table slouches, the guy over there sits up. Nobody sprawls. Also, and not least, there's your briefcase."

"I don't have a briefcase," Jeffords said.

"That's the point. The lawyers have briefcases," Meehan told him. "Old, battered, scuffed, packed full of paper. They're coming in for thirty seconds, tell you the delay was denied, we're going to trial Thursday, they're outta here, they still carry that briefcase. The *purpose* of that briefcase is to let you know, you're not the only scum they're taking care of around here, they don't have all that much time to spend on you. So for all of these many reasons, plus I notice you don't have your fingernails professionally attended to, you aren't a lawyer, and what that means is, we don't have a lawyer-client privilege."

Jeffords gazed on him in a dumbstruck way for a few seconds, as though listening to a simultaneous translation, and then a big goofy smile lit up his face, like a haunted house going up in flames just as the sun comes out, and he said, "Wow. Mr. Meehan, did I luck out with you."

And what was *that* supposed to mean? Sparrows take shit. Meehan could see this was gonna be a day of conundrums, and he could get along without such a day. If there was an up-side to jail time, it was at least you got some rest. He said, "Does this luck work both ways?"

"If you're as smart as you appear to be, yes." Suddenly businesslike, actually sitting upright, Jeffords opened the folder in front of himself, rested his forearms to flank the papers within, leaned forward like a bombardier, and read, "Francis Xavier Meehan, forty-two, no fixed abode."

"This place is pretty fixed," Meehan told him.

Jeffords looked up. "They call you Frank?"

"Never."

Jeffords waited, his silence inviting Meehan to tell him what "they" *did* call him, but Meehan didn't feel like getting into all that. Barbara used to call him Frannie, which nobody else did. When he was a kid he was mostly Francis, except a few of the guys he hung out with called him Zave, which followed through into the army and for a while after that. Now and again, somebody thought it was cute to nickname him Profes-sor, but it never took. The last ten, fifteen years he was called Meehan, which generally eliminated confusion.

Giving up without a fight, Jeffords bent his head to the folder: "Divorced from Barbara Kenilmore, two—"

"That's her maiden name."

Jeffords looked up. "She went back to it."

Meehan grinned. "That'll put me in my place," he said.

"You're already in your place," Jeffords told him, "but we'll see what we can do about it." He looked down again. "Two sons, Bri—"

"I know their names," Meehan said. "I even know their ages, their birthdays."

"We'll move along, then," Jeffords agreed.

Meehan said, "You're not gonna reel off my arrests and convictions, are you? I'll do what in court they say, stipulate. I'll stipulate to that. Many many burglary arrests, six, no seven trials, two convictions, lot of waiting time in places like this around the country because nobody ever thinks I'm worth bail—"

"Do *you* think you're worth bail?" Jeffords said.

Meehan had to laugh at that. "The judges would do it, don't get me wrong," he said. "It's the bondsmen. They look at me, they know they'd rather not have to find me."

Jeffords leaned back, morphing toward his natural sprawl. He said, "So we both know everything that's in here."

"Makes sense."

"But this is your first federal rap," Jeffords pointed out.

"I'm not glad I switched brands," Meehan told him, "if that's what you want to know."

Jeffords looked thoughtful, almost kindly. "Federal prisons," he said, "are not easy places."

"So I've heard."

"They've got you, you know," Jeffords said. "Witnesses, fingerprints—"

"It shouldn't be federal," Meehan insisted. "I'm not one to bitch against the system, but this is a fucking *truck*, Mr. Jeffords, supposed to be full of computer chips. This isn't blowing up army bases. This isn't even fucking stock fraud."

"The feds don't want to let you go," Jeffords said. He sounded as though he knew what he was talking about.

"Shit," Meehan said, and he meant it.

"Forever," Jeffords told him. "You're looking at life, no parole."

"For a truck."

"I wish I could help," Jeffords said.

Meehan gave him a keen look, while that sentence just lay there in the room with them. There's a reason we're having this conversation. He said, "Mr. Jeffords, I'm sorry, I feel awful about this, but I've just got this miserable memory. Already I'm starting to forget *your* name."

"No no, Frank," Jeffords said, "you've got—"

"Well, I suppose it had to happen," Meehan said.

Thrown off stride, Jeffords frowned at him: "What?"

"That somebody would call me Frank. Sure hope it doesn't happen again."

Jeffords took a slow half minute to think about whether he might get pissed off, then decided no, which Meehan found very interesting. This guy really wanted Meehan's cooperation. It was only too bad he had nothing to give him. I regret I have but one life to give for my federal penitentiary.

"Mr. Meehan," Jeffords said, "let me clear up any confusion between us."

"Go ahead," Meehan said.

"I'm not interested in the past," Jeffords said.

Was this another conundrum? Jail, courts, holding cells, the past was all they were ever about, because the future is already determined and set. Everybody knew Francis Xavier Meehan's future; they just had to tidy up his past before they could send him on to it.

While Meehan tried to work out what this was all about, Jeffords turned his notepad to another blank page, wrote in it fast, then turned it and the pen toward Meehan, who leaned closer to read

*If you might want to help me,*
*I might want to help you.*
YES ☐
NO ☐

Meehan studied this ballot, while Jeffords said, "If you could see your way clear to help the federal authorities on this hijacking case—"

Surprised, doubly surprised, Meehan looked up to see Jeffords' head shaking back and forth like a metronome while he talked: Ignore the words coming out of this mouth.

"—I think I might be able to help you in a variety of ways, particularly choice of penal institution, that sort of thing."

Meehan picked up the pen. "I'm really sorry, Mr. Jeffords," he said, "I just can't." He voted YES, a big X inside the box.

"Well, that's a shame," Jeffords said. "It was worth a try. Goodbye, Mr. Meehan."

"Goodbye, Mr. Jeffords."

# 3

THAT WAS THE afternoon 9 South had library privileges, three to five. Meehan had checked out the library when he'd first been tossed in here, but didn't think much of it, though everybody else loved the place, went there every chance they got.

Essentially, the inmates' part of the library was two rooms, the first a fairly big rectangle with two long library tables and some chairs, the walls lined with bookcases, the shelves full of fairly recent fiction and non-fiction, hardcover and paperback. There were no stacks, just the wall shelves, because stacks would give you a place to hide, exchange contraband, shiv an associate. That first room was where Meehan went, twice, to see what they had that might be of interest. Both times, he checked something out, only to realize he'd already read it.

The room beyond the normal library was the law library, which was smaller, with a wall-mounted shelf containing four electric typewriters on one side and a counter with a volunteer lawyer behind it on the other. Every typewriter always had an inmate banging away, with every range from two fingers to nine, while two or three behind him waited their turn. Behind the lawyer, out of sight back there, was another room—or maybe rooms—full of law books. The volunteer lawyer was there to answer questions, discuss situations, go back to find the relevant law books, Virgil the inmate through the narrow byways of the law.

This is where the inmates came to work on their cases. That's what they called it, they were working on their cases. Stick around in there long enough, you could come out with a pretty good grounding in tort law, which some of them did. But, since they were mostly assholes, it rarely helped. Still, working on their cases kept them out of trouble and made the volunteer lawyer—young, idealistic, from some seventh-rate diploma mill—feel useful in life.

Meehan didn't work on his case. He knew what his case was, and he knew working on it wouldn't make it any prettier. And he'd given up on the reading section of the library, as being too skimpy for his needs. So he was one of the few residents of 9 South present in his cell when the two guards came along, with that usual expression on their face—it's only the vow I made to the Blessed Virgin Mary keeps me from kicking your nose out the back of your head—and one of them said, "Meehan?"

"That's me," Meehan agreed.

"Pack your shit," the guard said. The other guard was there mostly, Meehan figured, to make sure the first guard kept his vow.

Meehan said, "Pack? Whadaya mean?"

"It means what you leave behind you leave behind," the guard told him. "What you take with you is still yours. Do it now, Meehan."

There wasn't much. He had a cheap blue nylon ditty bag, his toilet kit, socks and T-shirts and shorts, a couple shirts and pants he didn't put any wear on in here because everybody was in brown or orange jumpsuits (his was brown), the notebook he didn't write in—ten thousand rules—a couple paper-

backs that were personal property (*Under the Volcano* and
*Lord Jim*, neither of which he could get into, which was why
they were still with him, and which he figured was his fault,
not the writers'), and a pair of simple black laceless deck shoes
for when he had an exercise turn in the yard on the roof, shoes
generally called winos because that's who wears them.

Packing these worldly goods, Meehan said, "I'm packing.
Okay if I know where I'm going?"

"Otisville," the guard said. He didn't care.

Otisville. Meehan made a face, but didn't say anything.
What would he expect from these guys, sympathy?

Otisville was another more rural federal detention center in
this state. Since the criminal justice system around New York
City always gets such a heavy workout, the MCC here fre-
quently overflowed, like a cesspool, and then some of the contents had to be drained off to Otisville, one hundred miles
upstate in the Shawangunk Mountains, the middle of boonie
nowhere. A Department of Corrections bus, which looked like
a schoolbus except it was dark blue and had mesh cages over
all the windows, ran up to Otisville every evening, back down
every morning, four hours out of your day on the bus. Except
not until his trial; for now, they'd just ship him off to Otisville
and leave him there. But then, at trial time, as though it wasn't
tough enough to be on trial in a federal court, they'd throw in
this commute, just to help you keep on your toes.

Meehan packed everything into his ditty bag, put on the
zippered cotton jacket he'd worn when they'd picked him up,
and left his little cell for the last time. Out in the star chamber,
Johnson sat at a plastic table, cheating at solitaire. Looking up,
eying the guards, he said, "Hey. Where *you* going?"

"Otisville."

Johnson made a face. "Fuck me," he said.

"Yeah, well." Meehan saw no point in mentioning his sus-
picions of Johnson.

He and the guards went out to the elevators and rode down to 2, for his check-out, which consisted of impersonal clerks, a lot of paperwork, and a moment where, under everybody's indifferent eye, he changed out of their brown jumpsuit into his own gray work shirt and black chino pants.

At the end came the shackles. The shackles was a loose chain around the waist, with a short chain linking it to handcuffs and a longer chain linking it to ankle cuffs. Dressed like that, you shuffled, with your hands at your belt.

Another elevator took the three of them down to the loading dock and departure area, with a big broad opening onto St. George Place, the narrow one-way street at the back of the MCC. The Otisville bus was there, a dozen guys on line, shuffling forward with their hands at their belts, going through the cumbersome motions of climbing up into a bus with shackles on, looking like elephants climbing into a treehouse.

Meehan turned in that direction, the ditty bag bouncing against the front of his thighs, both hands holding the handle. He just had time to notice that all those guys were still in their orange or brown jumpsuits when the guard on that side of him gave him a poke on the shoulder and pointed. "That way."

What way? What other way was there? There was never anything but one way.

But why had they put him in civvies? Meehan looked where the guard pointed, and a small anonymous black sedan was there, within the loading area but pointed out, exhaust puffing from its tail pipe.

The devil you know. Meehan looked over his shoulder at what looked now like the safety of the Otisville bus, but shuffled the other way instead, toward the black sedan, trailed by the guards.

They approached the sedan from its right side, and as they got near, the front door on this side opened and a very tall skinny guy in a dark suit and tie and black topcoat got out. Not

quite looking at Meehan, he opened the rear door, and Meehan understood that was where he was supposed to go. He
shuffled to the car, paused to figure out how to get into the
back seat, and the tall skinny guy took the ditty bag from his
hands, saying, "Allow me," still not exactly looking at Meehan.

"Thanks."

Meehan bent down, to judge his approach, and was not
completely surprised to see Jeffords in there, smiling a welcome at him from the far side of the back seat.

# 4

ONCE MEEHAN MANAGED to get his shackled feet into the car and flat on the floor, the tall skinny guy shut his door and carried himself and Meehan's ditty bag to the front seat, where he put the bag on the floor next to his own feet, then shut his door. A solid *clunk* sounded inside the door beside Meehan, and, he realized, the same sound came from all the other doors as well. "So we're child-proof now," he said, and Jeffords chuckled.

They were four in the car, the other being the driver; what Meehan could see of him was meaty shoulders in dark wool, flat ears, fat rolls on the back of the neck, and a Dick Tracy hat squared off on his head. He lifted that head to look at Jeffords in the mirror and say, "All set?"

"Ready to roll," Jeffords told him.

The driver put the sedan in gear and drove out to St. George Place, where there was never any traffic, because it was a one-way street, it was one block long, and it went from nowhere to nowhere under the enclosed third-floor walkway that led from the MCC over to the courts. The driver steered them back into the world of streets that went somewhere, then

directly onto the Brooklyn Bridge; so long, Manhattan Correctional Center, and so long, Manhattan.

Meehan had assumed Jeffords would say something, this
being his party, but they were across the bridge and onto the
Brooklyn Queens Expressway, Long Island–bound, and Jeffords still did nothing but gaze kind of dreamily out at twilight
New York City, October of the year, Manhattan very dramatic
from here, so Meehan finally cleared his throat and rattled his
chains and said, "Uh, Mr. Jeffords."

Jeffords turned mild eyes his way. "Yes?"

Meehan rattled his chains again. "We're doing sixty," he
pointed out, "and the doors are double-locked. Do I have to
have these things on?"

Jeffords seemed surprised the shackles were still there. "No,
of course not," he said. "Jimmy," he called to the skinny guy
up front, "give me the key to these things."

Jimmy turned halfway around, showing Meehan his beaky
nose. "What things?"

"These, these chains things."

"Shackles," Meehan prompted.

"Shackles," Jeffords agreed. "Meehan doesn't need them
now, give me the key."

"*I* don't have the key," Jimmy said.

Jeffords was aghast. "You don't have the *key?*"

"No," Jimmy said. "Why would *I* have the key?"

Jeffords frowned at one of the driver's neck rolls. "Buster?
Do you have the key, to these cuff things?"

"I haven't carried cuff keys in eight years," the driver said,
confirming Meehan's suspicion the guy was an ex-cop. Not a
cop? An ex-cop? And Jeffords not a lawyer. He wondered what
Jimmy wasn't.

Smart. Jimmy said, "Should I radio?"

Jeffords hated that idea. "What? Radio who? You don't radio
in the New York City area, it's like a party line around here."

Jimmy said, "Maybe when you get to Norfolk—"

"Norfolk!" Everything Jimmy said appalled Jeffords. "We can't leave this man in chains all the way to Norfolk!"

Norfolk, Meehan thought. Isn't that in Virginia? What the hell am I gonna do in Norfolk?

"Buster," Jeffords said, leaning forward, speaking earnestly to Buster's neck rolls, "we've gotta go back."

Jimmy said, "Pat, you sure?" He still hadn't made direct eye contact with Meehan.

Buster said, "The plane—"

"It isn't a goddam scheduled flight," Jeffords snapped, "and yes, Jimmy, I'm sure. We're asking for this man's cooperation. We can't keep him chained up like a, a, a Doberman pinscher! Buster, turn us around, we'll drive back, wait for me out front on Park Row. I'll go in and get the key."

"You're the boss," Buster said, not as though he thought that was such a good thing.

"There's an exit up ahead," Jeffords said.

"I see it," Buster said.

Meehan was beginning to lose faith in these people.

# 5

THEY HAD TO unclunk the doors when they got to the main entrance to the MCC, in the gathering gloom of twilight. "Keep an eye on him," Jeffords advised, and climbed out of the car to trot over to and through the grim entrance, with its anti-suicide-truck row of round concrete posts along the sidewalk out front like parts of some low-tech board game, and the mirrored windows on the second floor, so you never knew who or what was watching.

Well, Jimmy was watching, keeping the eye on Meehan that Jeffords had ordered, but he didn't look comfortable about it, and he managed to do it while still avoiding eye contact. Meehan ignored him to look out at his former home, his fixed abode for the last eleven days.

The MCC was the Bastille writ small, the runt of the same litter, tall, dark, concrete, with rounded corners rather than sharp edges. It had a closed-in look, like the kind of maniac that listens to voices in his teeth a lot. When the French decided to give freedom a shot, they tore their Bastille down; when the Americans opted for freedom, they put up the MCC. Go figure.

Jeffords came trotting out of the building and toward the car, looking as though the structure hadn't harmed him very much in the three or four minutes he'd been inside. When he slid into the car, though, Meehan could see he was a bit ruffled, as though he'd had a conversation inside there that hadn't been completely pleasant. Trying to sound cheerful and confident, he said, "Okay, Buster, all set now," and as Buster silently sent them off into traffic, reheaded for the Brooklyn Bridge, Jeffords flashed the flat steel key and said, "Just a sec, now."

It took more than a sec, since Jeffords had clearly never had dealings with shackles before, but it didn't take long, and they were barely on the bridge before Meehan was rubbing his chafed wrists and moving his feet around just for the fun of it, saying, "Thanks. I appreciate that."

"Mr. Meehan," Jeffords said, "as I think you've already figured out, my job earlier today was to check you out, see if you were the man we want. That you're here shows my belief that you *are* the man we want. You just go on behaving like the intelligent guy I know you are, and you'll never see another shackle all your born days."

"That sounds good," Meehan said. "Of course, I don't know what you *mean* by the man you want. The man you want for what?"

Jeffords leaned a little closer, which Meehan didn't like, and murmured, "Not everybody in this car is cleared for this."

Since Meehan had no idea what "this" was, he assumed he was one of those in the car not cleared for it, so he decided to leave that alone, and say instead, "You were talking before about Norfolk. Going to Norfolk."

"That's right," Jeffords said, as though glad Meehan had reminded him of something important. "Now, on the plane," he said, "we should be the only passengers."

"Uh-huh."

"But it's a contributor's plane," Jeffords explained, "so you never know. So if there *is* somebody else there, or somebody in the crew says something to you, just go along with it."

"Sure," Meehan said.

"I doubt anybody will talk to you at all," Jeffords said. "But if anybody asks, you're an Internet technician."

It would be hard for Meehan to imagine anything further from himself than an Internet technician. He said, "What if they want to know what that means?"

Jeffords laughed. "Nobody wants to expose their ignorance," he said. "Just say you're working on the streaming technology on the Internet."

"The streaming technology on the Internet," Meehan echoed.

Up front, Jimmy showed his beaky profile again, saying, "Pat, do you really think he can bring that off?"

"I'm sure he can," Jeffords said.

Turning a bit farther, Jimmy almost but not quite made eye contact, his glance brushing across Meehan's cheek as he said, with what sounded a bit like petulance, "Of course, I'm not to know what we want him for—"

"All in good time, Jimmy," Jeffords assured him. "I know you, as much as anybody, understand the need for security here."

"I'm not asking," Jimmy said, and faced front, and Meehan caught Buster looking at him in the interior rearview mirror, a tight little smile on his bulldog face. Buster didn't need to know the details either; he already knew all he needed to know about Francis Xavier Meehan.

He did, too. Meehan looked away from those ex-cop eyes and out his window, to watch industrial Queens race by.

Contributor's plane. What the hell was a contributor's plane?

A CORPORATE JET.

Buster led them along unknown back alleys at JFK International airport, big planes hunched in the distance like dozing wasps, then angled around a chain-link fence to stop next to a sleek smallish jet that looked like a mini-Concorde. It was all white, and had only numbers on it, no names. The door in its side had been opened down to become the entrance stairs.

All four got out of the car, though two wouldn't be flying today, but everybody wanted to help watch Meehan. Jeffords, meeting him around the hood of the car, smiled cheerfully and gestured at the waiting plane. "You first."

"I know," Meehan said.

The interior was all carpet in different shades of ecru and beige and tan, floor and walls alike. There were eight low broad overstuffed beige armchairs in this mellow-lit tube, four on each side, each with its own portholish window and its own side table. And in the first chairs, to right and left, were people.

The more interesting one was the woman on the right, a big-chested ash blonde of not yet thirty with very red lipstick and a very short pink skirt. Eleven days in the slammer can be a long time, sometimes.

So she was the more interesting one, but the more important one was clearly the man on the left. Maybe fifty, gym-trim, almost completely bald except for a low-lying hedge of black, dressed in tassel loafers and knife-edge slacks and a gray-blue sports jacket over a blue-black polo shirt, he looked at the world through pale blue tinted designer spectacles and he gave off, from the first second you looked at him, an air of absolute self-assurance so total your first reaction was to kick him in the nuts just to see what he'd do.

This fellow offered Meehan a tight unpleasant smile, as though daring him to kick him in the nuts, and said, "I guess you're who we're waiting for."

"I guess so," Meehan said, as Jeffords bounded up and into the plane, saying, "Hi, there," extending his hand, saying, "Pat Jeffords."

"Howie Briggs," the guy answered, not standing, but accepting the handshake, clearly seeing that Jeffords, like himself, was the more important member of the duo. "And this is Cindy."

"Hi," said Cindy, in the kind of voice she would have.

"Arthur wanted us to hitch a ride," Howie Briggs said, "meet him down at Hilton Head."

"I envy you," Jeffords said, with a happy smile. "And this is Frank."

"How are you?"

"Good," Meehan said.

Jeffords might be irritating with the "Frank" business, but in some ways he seemed to know what he was doing. For instance, he seated himself behind Howie Briggs and Meehan behind Cindy, so it would be harder for Briggs to engage Meehan in conversation. And Cindy, of course, would know better than to engage anybody but Briggs in conversation, so it was unlikely Meehan would have to demonstrate for anybody his expertise in streaming technology on the Internet.

The plane jolted forward, to start what would eventually turn out to be a very long taxi, and Meehan settled down, grinning a little, thinking this place was a lot better than the place he'd come from. Also, he discovered, the seat swiveled.

Keen.

# 7

In Norfolk, it was totally night. Full of macadamia nuts and club soda, Meehan stepped down from the contributor's plane (still had no idea what *that* meant) in this remote corner of Norfolk International to find *two* Busters in topcoats and Dick Tracy hats waiting for him at the foot of the stairs. A little way off, Howie Briggs and Cindy were getting into a white limo. Behind Meehan, Jeffords came cheerfully down the stairs and said, "Well, let's go. Where's our transportation?"

"There, sir," said one of the Busters, pointing.

"Good. Let's do it."

Without anybody saying anything one way or another, the new Busters walked to either side of Meehan, with Jeffords coming along behind. They moved toward the white limo, which then drove away, to reveal another black sedan parked beyond it, but this one larger and newer-looking than the one in New York. A Buster held the rear door open, and Meehan entered, followed by Jeffords. The Buster shut the door, the two Busters got in front, and the drive began.

There was very little conversation over the next hour and a half, except when Meehan said, "One thing."

Jeffords raised an eyebrow at him. "Mm?"

"You introduce me to one other person as Frank," Meehan told him, "whatever it is you want me to do, I won't do it. I'll go back to the MCC first."

"I didn't know it was that important to you," Jeffords said.

"Neither did I."

"Okay, fine." In pale dashboard light from up front, Jeffords' face looked as innocent as a statue in church. "So what do you prefer?" he asked. "I mean, I can't just introduce you as Meehan."

"I'll take Francis," Meehan said.

"That's a good name," Jeffords allowed. "A little more ambiguous, you know what I mean, but good. Okay, it's a deal."

Thinking he might be on a roll, Meehan said, "Will you tell me where we're going?"

"Outer Banks," Jeffords said, with a blank smile, and looked out his window at blackness, since they'd left Norfolk behind some time ago.

Outer Banks. That was an answer, and yet it wasn't an answer, so Meehan contented himself with the fact that he wouldn't be Franked any more.

Hour and a half, maybe a little longer, and they stopped in the darkness at a gate and a guard shack, with tall razor-wire-topped chain-link fence stretched away to left and right. A guard in a greenish brown uniform came out of the shack, looking doubtful. The Buster at the wheel slid his window down to show a paper to the guard, who took it and carried it with him to his shack.

The Buster said over his shoulder to Jeffords, "He's phoning."

"They should have put us on the list," Jeffords said. He sounded annoyed.

Meehan looked out at the sign on the wall of the shack,

under the windows. Something about United States Government, and big block letters N P S.

The guard returned, less dubious but no more friendly. He
gave the Buster back his paper, and went away to electrically
open the gate. They drove through, and Meehan felt the
guard's intense stare on his cheek on the way by.

From here, the road, two-lane concrete, meandered along,
and Meehan became aware of buildings to both sides, all of
them dark. Then there was a lit-up one ahead on the right, a
blocky barrackslike place, four stories high, with a few windows lit on all the floors, and that's where they were headed.

Again the Buster escort as they walked up a concrete path
with lawn on both sides to the building entrance, where a
young woman in sweater and slacks, looking nervous, held the
door open and said, "I'm sorry, Mr. Jeffords, they were supposed to have been informed."

"No problem," Jeffords told her, in a tight-lipped way to let
her know it was a lie. "Where's our friend staying?"

"Four-twelve, sir."

Meehan hadn't realized "our friend" meant himself until Jeffords turned, handed him his ditty bag, gave him his usual
cheery smile, and said, "I'll see you in the morning, Francis.
These fellas will show you to your room."

"But—" said Meehan to Jeffords' back, as he walked off
down the hall with the worried young woman.

"We take the stairs," said a Buster.

Maybe it actually was a barracks; wide central hall to left
and right, wide iron stairs leading up, with a landing halfway.
Meehan and the Busters clanged up these stairs to the top and
along the hall to a brown metal door bearing a brass 412. A
key was stuck into the lock in the knob.

A Buster pulled open the door and said, "They'll call you
when they want you."

"I never ate dinner," Meehan said.

"They do big breakfasts around here," the other Buster told him.

The first Buster said, "I think there's snacks or something in there. Take a look."

No choice. Meehan stepped through the doorway, and the door snicked shut behind him. Click-click, went the key out there.

Room 412 was a plain but good bedroom; a lot better than 9 South. It was like a Holiday Inn room without the television set. The attached bath provided razor, toothbrush and toothpaste, and anything else he might need.

Also, there was food of a sort, on the metal table against the right wall, the double bed being against the left. The food was a bowl of apples and pears, a basket of different kinds of crackers and processed cheeses in individual clear packaging, and small bottles of apple juice and tomato juice and seltzer.

Meehan dropped his ditty bag on the bed, grabbed an apple, and went over to look out one of the two wide windows, having to lift a venetian blind out of the way. Down below was the road he'd come in. As he chewed and watched, the Busters came out and got into their car and drove off.

Okay, what does this door look like? Meehan tossed his apple core in the direction of the wastebasket and walked over to study the egress. Door opens outward, so there's no way to get at the hinges. Lock mounted into the knob on the outside, with no parts visible on the inside. Metal frame with a narrow lip extending over the front edge of the door.

So we are not going out that way. Meehan went into the bathroom instead, where he found the plumbing service panel low on the wall between the sink and the shower stall. A pop-top ring from one of the soda cans on the table opened the four Phillips-head screws, and the panel came off to reveal white plastic piping with blue or green taps and, as he'd hoped, another panel on the far side for access from the next-door bathroom.

Unfortunately, the space was too small and the pipes too many and too thick. He could get a foot through to kick out that other panel, but he'd never get his body through that twisty little space.

Discouraged, he got to his feet and went back to look at the main room. The two sheets on the bed were about five too few to reach from here to the ground even if he could get the window open and even if he felt like playing apeman, which he didn't. Walls, floor, and ceiling were featureless except for that impassable door.

Well, it looked as though he'd be spending the night.

THE PHONE HAD a British sound—*bzzt-bzzt*—rather than the American *braaang*. It startled Meehan awake, and he had no idea where he was or what that sound was or why he was seeing daylight through venetian blinds or why the *bzzt-bzzt* wouldn't stop. But then it did stop, when he found the phone on the metal bedside table, and put the receiver to his face, and said, "Whuzz."

"Oh eight hundred, sir," said a chipper female voice. "You'll be called for at oh eight-thirty."

"Uhh," Meehan said, and the phone answered with a dial tone, so he hung up.

By oh eight-thirty, he was showered and dressed and had eaten a pear. Nobody in his entire life before had ever said anything like "oh eight hundred" or "oh eight-thirty" in his presence, and he found he didn't like it. It made him nervous.

Click-click, went a key outside the door, which then opened, to show Jeffords himself, in different shirt and jacket but the same smile. Meehan looked past him, saw Jeffords was alone, but then realized he wasn't up to an escape attempt at this moment. Maybe after breakfast.

"Sleep well, Francis?"

"Oh, yeah. Thanks."

Clang-clang down the stairs they went, to the first floor, and down the hall to the very last door at the end, which opened to a very large office, extending from front to back across the end of the building, windows on three sides. The office was in segments, a desk segment to the left, a conference table segment to the right, a couches-and-armchairs conversation segment in the middle. A tall distinguished silver-haired man who looked like a Shakespearean actor or possibly a stock swindler stood up from the sweeping broad desk in the desk segment and said, "Ah, good morning. Just in time for breakfast. Sit down, you two, I'll make the call."

"Thanks, Bruce," Jeffords said, with a little wave, and told Meehan, "We'll sit here."

So they sat on couches in the conversation segment while Bruce murmured into his phone at his desk, and then Bruce came over to join them, so they stood up again and Jeffords said, "Francis Meehan, may I present Bruce Benjamin."

"How are you," Meehan said, and Bruce Benjamin said, "Delighted. Do sit down," so they all sat down again.

Benjamin had an avuncular smile that really cared about *you*, and really wanted to sell you some stock. "Good flight?" he asked.

"Sure."

"They treating you well here at— Oh, good," he said, and popped up again, because two black waiters in white had just wheeled in a table full of breakfast things: hot things like pancakes and scrambled eggs with Sterno cans under them, cold things like sliced melon and little corn flakes boxes, plus two kinds of coffee.

"Lovely," Benjamin told the waiters, who went away, and Benjamin said, "Why don't we eat while we chat?"

That seemed like a good idea. They filled plates and cups,

sat again, and Benjamin said, "I suppose you're wondering what this is all about."

"Most people would," Meehan suggested.

"Of course they would. It's quite simple," Benjamin assured him, which was what Meehan had been afraid of. "You are, if you don't mind my saying so, a thief."

"I don't mind you saying so *here*," Meehan told him.

"Of course." Benjamin had a store of meaningless smiles, like Halloween masks. He showed another from the collection and said, "Except for the occasional misfortune to which we are all heir—"

"Amen," said Jeffords.

"—it would seem you are quite an accomplished thief."

"Thank you," Meehan said. His jaws chewed toast while his mind worked like mad but went nowhere, like a squirrel in a wheel-shaped cage. What did these people want, and what could Meehan give them instead?

"As you have no doubt presumed," Benjamin went on, "we find ourselves in need of your skills."

"Talents," Jeffords said, around omelet. "Expertise."

"That, too," Benjamin said. "There is a certain place we wish you to enter," he explained, "and a certain object we wish you to collect, and turn over to us. You understand, there is much about this affair that must remain sub rosa."

"From me, you mean," Meehan said.

"Well, yes."

Spreading jam on toast, Jeffords said, "It's what we call a need-to-know basis."

"What *you* need to know," Benjamin told Meehan, "is that we are sufficiently connected to your government, in one way or another, that we can guarantee, if you accomplish this retrieval for us, your current troubles with the law will disappear."

"Never to return," Jeffords added.

"Well, *those* never to return," Benjamin cautioned. "Your future activities are out of our purview."

"So it's easy, isn't it?" Jeffords said. "We'll give you maps, we'll drive you to the place—"

"Near the place," Benjamin corrected.

"Well, sure," Jeffords agreed. "You go in, you get it, you bring it out, you give it to us, you're home free."

Meehan said, "Where is it, what is it, who's protecting it, what do you want with it, and who else wants it?"

"Sorry," Jeffords said, not sounding sorry at all. "Those are not within your need to know. The *where*, of course, you'll learn when we go there. But the point is, Francis, once you've done this simple little task, your days in the MCC are *over.*"

A big beaming smile on his face, the most impressive in his entire Halloween mask collection, Benjamin said, "So there you are. What do you say?"

"No," Meehan said.

THEY GAPED AT him. They couldn't believe it. "But," Benjamin said, "we're offering you your freedom."

"I doubt that all to hell," Meehan told him. "The way you birds operate, all you're offering me is additional charges."

Benjamin appealed to Jeffords. "You've talked to the man before," he said. "You recommended him. What's wrong? What does he want?"

"I don't know." A piece of bacon held forgotten in his upraised hand, like a baton, Jeffords mused at Meehan. Finally he said, "Do you *want* to go back to the MCC?"

"Yes."

"I can't believe that," Jeffords said. "It's a terrible place. You've said so yourself."

"It's a chrome cesspit," Meehan said. That was another of the ten thousand rules: Write poetry, but not *down.*

"Very good," Benjamin said; an aesthete, with a good ear.

"So," Jeffords insisted, "given it's . . . what you said, *why* would you want to go back there?"

"Because," Meehan explained, "they know what they're doing."

That stopped them both for a few seconds, while they gave one another bleak looks; no more smiles out of the Halloween trunk. Then Jeffords sighed and said, "You don't think we know what we're doing."

"Right."

"May I ask why?"

Meehan shrugged. "If you want to be insulted," he said, "that's up to you."

"Fire away," Jeffords said, but he looked a little pale.

Meehan nodded at him. "When you first showed up, you claimed you were a lawyer, and you couldn't make that one fly for five seconds. Do you think I was the only one in that building made you for a ringer?"

Stiffly, Jeffords said, "I wouldn't know."

"I would," Meehan said. "Then the next thing, you take me out of the MCC like it's a treat or something, but nobody thought about the key for the shackles. Then—"

Benjamin, taken aback, said, "Shackles?"

"There was a mix-up about the key," Jeffords mumbled. "We had to go back for it."

"I see." Benjamin nodded at Meehan. "Go on," he said.

"The next thing that happens," Meehan went on, "you got people on the plane that shouldn't be on the plane and shouldn't know there's anything funny going on, but they're on the plane because it's a contributor's plane, whatever that is, but whatever it is it means you don't control the situation. But if you're going to pull something with legal consequences, which is what you're talking about here, you've got to be able to control the situation."

Sounding frosty, Benjamin said, "I couldn't agree more, Mr. Meehan. Anything else?"

"Yes," Meehan said, marking that "Mr." "We get to the gate to this place out there last night and the guard doesn't know we're coming, so once again a whole lot of people who aren't supposed to know I'm here *do* know, because they have to be alerted before we can get in. I won't even talk about how I never got dinner. All I'll say is, you people tell me you picked me in particular to go into this caper with you, whatever it is, and I'm supposed to feel all honored and plucked-from-the-crowd, but what I tell you is, I wouldn't pick you to go to the deli with. So just take me back to the MCC."

Jeffords shook his head. "I never expected anything like this for a second," he said. He gazed at Meehan more in sorrow than in anger, a man whose pet dog won't do his great trick in front of company.

Benjamin, frowning deeply, said, "They didn't give you dinner?"

"There was fruit and stuff in the room," Meehan assured him, because he didn't want to make a huge complaint about it. He wanted either for these people to come clean, or to take him back to the MCC, and probably both. Whatever they had in mind, it seemed to Meehan much better than even money that they'd get caught doing it. What good was freedom, if it came attached to disaster?

"The interesting thing," Benjamin said to Jeffords, breaking a silence with which Meehan had been very comfortable, "is that we now have what I would call a very clear demonstration that we were right in the first place."

"I suppose so," Jeffords said, though he sounded gloomy about it.

"Pat," Benjamin said, "look on the bright side. You *did* pick the right man, and he has already proved that we do need such a person."

"Well," Jeffords said, with a sigh, "I do look pretty clumsy there, don't I, seen in the clear light of day."

"Because *that's* not what you're good at, Pat," Benjamin told him, back to being avuncular. "What *you're* good at is logistics, moving people and funds and transport in an open, clearcut, aboveboard manner."

"Filling out reports," Jeffords added, a bit resentfully, "every bloody step of the way."

"Precisely. You are not a thief," Benjamin went on, "and nor am I. And nor is anyone else in the committee, nor anyone we are likely to know. We were right to outsource, and now we must follow through."

Jeffords sighed. "Not what I expected," he said, "but I must agree. You know best."

"Thank you, Pat." Benjamin turned his benevolent gaze on Meehan. "In truth, we wish to put you in the position of our vendor in this matter, and we now realize, which I'm sorry we didn't realize before, that as our vendor, it is necessary that you be put in the picture."

"Hit me," Meehan said.

# 10

FIRST THEY ALL had to fortify themselves with provisions: sausages and toast for Benjamin, two kinds of melon for Jeffords, and more black coffee for Meehan, who wanted his wits somewhere he could find them without trouble.

At last, they were ready. "As you know," Benjamin began, "here we are, coming down to the wire in the election campaign, and—" He broke off, frowned at the expression on Meehan's face, and said, "The election campaign. The reelection of the president."

"*You* know," Jeffords encouraged.

"I've been kinda busy," Meehan reminded them. "Though, yeah, I guess I did see some headlines."

Benjamin was having trouble believing this. "Man, are you telling me you didn't *know* the president of the United States is running for reelection?"

"I don't usually pay that much attention to politics," Meehan admitted.

Benjamin gave Jeffords a helpless look. "You try and you try," he said, "to get your story out there."

"I know," Jeffords said, sounding sympathetic. "And every time, it's eighty-five percent didn't know a thing about it."

"I must admit, there are moments," Benjamin said, "I have my doubts about democracy. But you know what Churchill said."

"Of course," Jeffords said.

Meehan didn't know what Churchill said, but he was afraid, if he asked, Benjamin might start to cry, so he kept his mouth shut.

Benjamin took a deep breath and a forkful of scrambled egg, and then apparently felt better, because he said, "Well, let me be the first to tell you, Francis, there *is* a presidential election campaign under way even as we speak, and it's moving into an extremely critical phase—"

"Last minute," Jeffords said.

"That, too," Benjamin said. "And you, Francis, if you so choose, can be a significant factor in how this election works itself out."

They didn't bring me all this way to ask me to register to vote, Meehan told himself. "I wouldn't mind being a good citizen," he allowed.

"I was sure that's how you'd feel," Benjamin told him. "Now, Mr. Jeffords and I are, apart from other things, members of the CC, and we—"

Jeffords said, "Wait, Bruce," and to Meehan, "the Campaign Committee. We're part of the team to help reelect the president."

"Got it," Meehan said.

"Good," Benjamin said. "Now we have learned, fortuitously and fortunately, that there is a piece of very bad evidence in existence—"

"Videotaped confession," Jeffords put in, "supporting documents."

"Exactly," Benjamin said. "Extremely dangerous material in re POTUS. We have to—"

"Whoa," Meehan said. "Could you back to the last traffic light?"

Jeffords said, "POTUS is president of the United States."

"Yeah? Sounds more stupid that way."

Reproving, Benjamin said, "We think it lends a homey touch."

Meehan shrugged. "Okay."

Jeffords said, "The point is, the Other Side has this material, and we very much need to get it away from them."

Meehan said, "But they've already got it? For how long?"

"Two months," Benjamin said, "possibly a bit more."

"We just learned about it," Jeffords added, "this week."

Meehan said, "And they're just sitting on it? What are they gonna do, blackmail?"

Benjamin said, "No, no, that's not the way it works. They're waiting for an October Surprise."

Meehan shook his head. "I don't know what that is."

Jeffords explained, "Elections are held early in November. You hit the other side late in October with some really bad press, they don't have time to counteract it."

Meehan said, "Counteract? If this is such hot stuff, how do you counteract?"

"Given time, Francis," Benjamin said, "and the spin doctors at our command, we could counteract the crucifixion of Jesus Christ and you'd *vote* for Pontius Pilate."

Jeffords said, "That's why they save the Surprises for October. No time to massage the news."

"This is October," Meehan pointed out.

Benjamin said, "And now we come to you."

# 11

"You want me to get it," Meehan said.

"As I said," Benjamin agreed.

"With our assistance," Jeffords pointed out.

"There, you see," Meehan said, "there's our problem."

Benjamin said, "*Our* problem?"

"You don't trust me," Meehan told him, "and you're right. You give me a doorway and a running start and I'm outa here."

Drily, "We know that," Jeffords said.

"We all know that, or I wouldn't mention it. On the other hand," Meehan said, "I don't do my best work with amateurs in the room."

Jeffords, again on the edge of being miffed, said, "Meaning?"

"It's the old carpenter-to-homeowner wage scale," Meehan explained. "Twenty-five dollars an hour to do the job, thirty-five if you watch, forty-five if you help. I don't want you to watch, and I *sure* don't want you to help. So you'll have to leave me alone to do it my own way, and as soon as you do, I'm outa here." Meehan spread his hands. "I'm sorry, but there it is. I'd lie to you if I could, but we all know the situation."

Tentatively, Benjamin said, "A mere observer could—"

Meehan shook his head.

Benjamin and Jeffords frowned at one another, baffled. Jeffords said, "He refuses to do it if we observe, but he says himself if we let him out of our sight, he'll disappear, so he *still* won't do it."

Meehan wished he could help here, because he really *didn't* want life in a federal pen, but what was the alternative? In truth, Francis Xavier Meehan, though very bright, did not know how to think ahead. Witness his ruined marriage, his not very stellar criminal career, his very presence in the MCC. If he'd had a motto, other than the ten thousand rules, which was more mantra than motto, it would have been "one problem at a time."

Most of the guys he knew were the same. The people who thought ahead were the ones with the jobs and the mortgages and the car payments and the Tuesday night bowling leagues—how could Meehan *ever* know for sure where he'd be on a given Tuesday night?—whereas the guys like Meehan got whatever was going by.

He said, "Maybe . . ."

They both looked alert. Everybody in the room, including Meehan, waited to hear what he was going to say next.

"Maybe I could give you advice," he said.

Jeffords, looking insulted again, said, "Advice? About what?"

"About the heist. You keep me here, tell me the setup, I'll give you the best advice I got, very professional, you go collect your Surprise, and then we shake hands and I walk away."

Jeffords and Benjamin exchanged a look. "Not exactly what we had in mind," Benjamin said.

"But the only possibility, apparently," Jeffords said. "And if we put this one back, look for another one, that's *more* time gone, and maybe second-best. And we do have people willing to go in and do it."

"Willing, yes," Benjamin said, and shrugged. "All right, we'll try it." Turning to Meehan, he said, "The gentleman who now has the package is a supporter of the president's challenger, the candidate on the Other Side. In fact, a very large contributor to his campaign."

"A contributor's plane," Meehan said, dawn breaking. "Now I get it."

"Yes, of course," Benjamin agreed. "*This* contributor, however, is one of theirs, from a fine old Revolutionary-era family—"

"Many of them on the wrong side even then," Jeffords added snidely, "though they don't talk about that much any more."

"Nevertheless," Benjamin said, "he is noted for his collection of antique firearms, exclusively from the periods of our Revolution, the War of 1812, and the Civil War. A well-known collection, occasionally on tour to American Legion posts, private schools, that sort of thing."

"And when it's at home," Meehan said, "I bet they keep it locked up, being guns and all. And your package is in there with it."

"Exactly."

"So is it in the guy's house, or a separate building, or what does he— Wait a minute."

They looked at him. Benjamin said, "Yes?"

"Just a minute," Meehan said. "I think maybe I can do it for you."

Jeffords said, "Do it?"

"Get you your package." Meehan grinned at them. "Yeah, I think maybe so, maybe after all I can help you guys out."

# 12

"I'm gonna need two things," Meehan told them. "A pay phone, and my lawyer."

Jeffords said, "A pay phone? What do you mean, a pay phone?"

"A phone you put money in," Meehan explained.

"I know *that*," Jeffords said. "But if you want a phone—"

"Security," Benjamin gently told Jeffords. "He wants to make a secure call."

"Well, there is no such thing," Jeffords said.

"Some are more secure than others," Meehan told him.

Benjamin said, "If you don't mind the question, who is it you wish to call?"

"The guy who takes stuff off my hands."

Benjamin nodded. "A fence, you mean."

"I know he can take computer chips," Meehan said, "and I know he can take furs, and I know he can take oriental rugs. Muskets and blunderbusses, I dunno. I gotta ask him."

"My God," Benjamin said, getting it, "you mean to steal the man's guns!"

"Well, sure," Meehan agreed. "That's what makes me stick

around. I go in, even without you people watching me, I go in and I get your package, and while I'm there I pick up some stuff for myself."

Benjamin said, "You're telling us you mean to commit a burglary! And you're *telling* us!"

"Mr. Benjamin," Meehan said, "it was always gonna be a burglary. Didn't you know that? Somebody breaks in and takes away something doesn't belong to them, that's a burglary."

"But not for *profit*," Benjamin insisted. "What we're talking about is politics."

"Dirty tricks," Jeffords added.

"Exactly," Benjamin said.

"Well, I only work for profit," Meehan told him. "So I'll give you your choice. I'll stay here if you want, give you advice, you go in and do your best, maybe it'll work out, or maybe the papers get full of the president's campaign committee arrested for housebreaking."

"Oh, God," Benjamin said.

"Or," Meehan went on, "you give me the layout, I go in, I get you your package, I pick up my profit at the same time."

Benjamin said, "Pat? What do you think?"

"I think," Jeffords said, "the man is asking us to be accessories to a felony."

Meehan said, "It always was a felony. Breaking and entering."

"Well, it didn't *feel* like a felony," Jeffords said.

"In my experience," Meehan told him, "cops don't go by feelings."

"Well, Pat," Benjamin said, "we wanted a professional, and I'd say we got one."

Jeffords looked bleak. "You want to go along with him."

"We told each other, Pat," Benjamin said, "that what went wrong with the Watergate burglary years ago was that it was performed by amateurs. Ideologues, spies, political henchmen.

Not a professional thief in the crowd. We told each other we should learn from that experience. Thus Francis Meehan. And thus, our burglary turns, I'm afraid, into an actual burglary."

Jeffords sighed. "Agreed," he said, though without joy.

Benjamin turned to Meehan. "What was the other? A lawyer? Francis, what do you want with a lawyer?"

"I wouldn't negotiate with you people without one," Meehan said. "If we're gonna get serious here."

"Very well," Benjamin said. "Who is this lawyer?" And he made himself ready to take a note.

"Goldfarb," Meehan told him. "Wait a minute, Eileen? No. Elaine! Elaine Goldfarb."

Sounding outraged, as though someone were pulling his leg, Jeffords said, "Elaine Goldfarb? She's your court-appointed attorney at the MCC!"

Meehan shrugged. "What other lawyer am I gonna have?"

Benjamin said, "You don't want some public defender hack, Francis. If you feel you need an attorney, and you may be right about that, I wouldn't argue the issue, we can surely find you one in the greater DC area who would—"

"Yeah," Meehan said, "and I know where you'd find him, too. Not very far down in your pocket. The great thing about Elaine Goldfarb is, I *know* she isn't one of yours."

"Certainly not," Jeffords said.

"Very well," Benjamin said. "We'll see what we can do about a secure telephone and obtaining the services of Ms. Goldfarb. She won't be licensed in the state of Virginia, you realize."

"If I have to take you birds to court," Meehan told him, "I'll get somebody local."

His smile thin, Benjamin said, "Yes, that would be a new role in court for you, wouldn't it? In the meantime, if you've done breakfast . . ."

"Long ago," Meehan said.

"Fine." The smile turning sad, Benjamin said, "I am sorry, but I know you understand, you'll have to return to your room awhile. There are magazines on that table over there, you're welcome to take some with you."

They all stood. "It's a boring room," Meehan said. "I just wanna mention that."

"We'll make your stay in it as short as possible," Benjamin promised. "In fact, I'll hope to see you in the cafeteria at lunch."

"I think I can probably make it," Meehan said.

# 13

AT LUNCH, IN another room in the same building, this one a plain bright cafeteria on the second floor with much the same view as everywhere else in this place, surrounded by people in olive drab uniforms or scruffy civvies, everybody carrying around brown trays with blah food on them, Benjamin said, "It's all worked out."

Meehan looked up from studying his cheeseburger. "What is?"

"Ms. Goldfarb will arrive at Norfolk International at two thirty-five this afternoon," Benjamin said. "You will meet her."

"With an escort," Jeffords added.

"I know," Meehan said, around the cheeseburger, which tasted better than it looked.

"While at the airport," Benjamin went on, "you will be able to make a phone call from any one of the pay phones there, with your escort nearby but not listening."

"Sounds good," Meehan said. "I'll need change," he said, and bit into more cheeseburger.

Benjamin blinked. "Change?"

Jeffords explained, "They don't have cash money in the MCC."

"Oh, of course." Benjamin turned politely to Meehan. "How much?"

His mouth full of cheeseburger, Meehan raised his left hand and splayed the fingers out twice.

Benjamin's look turned sardonic. "Ten dollars? I think not. Jeffords will give you three."

Neither Meehan nor Jeffords was happy about that.

Meehan kept an eye on the route, in case he ever had to take it on his own some time; another of the ten thousand rules. Grandy, Currituck, Moyock; the town names in North Carolina were weird, but somehow not easy to remember. Then they crossed into Virginia and got Hickory and Great Bridge, and there they were on Battlefield Boulevard; can't these people get over it? Battlefield Boulevard led them to an interstate, which snaked them through Norfolk to the airport, right in the middle of town.

It was the same car as last night, with the same team; Jeffords next to Meehan in back, the two Busters up front. They'd changed their shirts, but not their topcoats and squared-off hats.

From the parking lot, they moved like a highly trained close-drill team into the terminal building where, amid the announcements and the lost children and the teenagers traveling with their skateboards, Jeffords grudgingly counted out three dollars in quarters and dimes and nickels into Meehan's palm. "Thanks, Dad," Meehan said, and Jeffords gave him a sour look.

The bank of pay phones was clustered in a little campground of its own off to the side of pedestrian traffic. One Buster stood off to the right, the other equally to the left, and

Jeffords paced back and forth in the near distance, getting in the way of people carrying heavy luggage.

By necessity, Meehan's telephone directory was kept in his head. He dialed the number, pumped in change, and the nasal voice that he knew was female only because he'd seen its owner a few times over the years said, "Cargo." Cargo Storage was the name under which Leroy worked.

"Leroy, please."

"Who shall I say?"

"Meehan." It always bothered Meehan to speak his name aloud on the telephone, but sometimes you had to.

"Leroy isn't in at the moment," she said, which is what he'd known she would say. "Can he get back to you?"

"I'm at a pay phone at Norfolk International Airport," Meehan told her.

"What a weird place to be."

"You don't know the half of it," he said, and read the number off to her, and hung up.

Both Busters immediately moved toward him, but he held up both hands, one to either side, to deter them, so they backed off to position A, glancing toward Jeffords to be sure it was okay.

Meehan pretended to be actively using the phone for the next seven minutes, holding the receiver to his ear while keeping the hook depressed with his other hand. Then at last, once Leroy had reached his own secure phone, this one rang. Meehan lifted the hook, and a different nasal voice said in his ear, "What the fuck you doin in Norfolk fuckin Virginia?"

"I hope to tell you some day," Meehan said. "For right now, I want to know, if I happened to come into possession of some antique guns, all American, Revolution, Civil War, would you be interested?"

"Antique guns? So you mean a collection."

"Yeah."

"Lemme think, lemme think. Is it Lewes-Moday?"

"What?"

"Which collection is it? Who owns it?"

"I dunno yet."

"You're a strange bird, Meehan," Leroy told him. "When you find out whose house you're in, call me back."

"No, hold on, I'll find out." Gesturing to Jeffords, he said into the phone, "What was that name you said?"

"Lewes-Moday. If it's Lewes-Moday, I don't want it. They got photos of every fucking piece, they injected bird DNA in the stocks, nobody's gonna dare go near a piece of that."

"Okay, hold on." To Jeffords, now next to him frowning deeply, he said, "Whose collection is this?"

Jeffords looked shocked, then mulish. "I can't tell you that, not at this point."

"Is it Lewes-Moday? Just tell me if it's Lewes-Moday."

"I've never heard of Lewes-Moday," Jeffords said, as though he felt obscurely as though he'd been accused of something.

Into the phone, Meehan said, "It isn't Lewes-Moday. What I think it is, I think it's somebody in the northeast, a rich guy, political, probably an estate or some—"

"Oh, Burnstone!" Leroy said. "Absolutely! You get your hands on Burnstone, you got a deal."

"One second." Meehan looked at Jeffords, who was practicing his poker face. Looking deep into those eyes, Meehan said, "Burnstone."

"I can't tell you—"

Meehan said into the phone, "It's Burnstone. See you soon."

# 14

HER PLANE WAS thirty-five minutes late, which isn't bad for an airplane, and at first he didn't recognize her among the passengers drifting brain-damaged into the terminal. He'd only seen Elaine Goldfarb three times in his life, always in the MCC, she on the other side of the black metal desk, dressed like a yak, so it took a few seconds to realize that *this* woman was *that* woman.

She presented herself differently out here; not more attractive, more aggressive. Her skinny body was encased in fairly tight black slacks and clacking black leather boots and a gleaming black leather jacket, with an open zipper. Her steel-wool hair was controlled by a golden barrette at the back in the shape of a narrow bouquet of roses, and large gold hoop earrings dangled to both sides of that sharp-nosed sharp-jawed face, making her black-framed eyeglasses look more than ever like spy holes in a fortress wall.

So this is how she dresses to go on the road; challenging. Don't dare fuck with me. Interesting. A woman wouldn't want to offer any challenges in the MCC.

She had as much trouble recognizing him as he'd had with

her, apparently, because she looked right through him until he raised his hand as though to attract teacher's attention. But that was okay; again, the context was different. She'd only seen him in the brown jumpsuit, probably looking as crappy and defeated as he'd then felt. Out here, in his own clothes, with a little scheme working, operating with people who turned about as rapidly as a battleship, he not only felt better, he no doubt looked better as well. Other, anyway. So he raised his hand, and when she furrowed her high brow at him he said, "Yeah, it's me, after all."

So she came over to him, there in the middle of the terminal, people all over the place going on about their own business, and she said, "You're *out?*"

"Kinda," he said.

"Francis Meehan," she said, as though to double-check her data.

"The same," he agreed.

"You want to be called Meehan."

"Yes, thank you."

"Well, you're the last person I expected to see here," she said. "I'll call you Meehan if you'll tell me *what* the hell is going on."

"Listen," he said, "could you spring for coffee? They only gave me three bucks, and it's gone, and it's okay if we go to the coffee shop and sit down and get on the same page here."

"Everything you're saying," she told him, "comes within a whisker of making sense."

"Coffee," he said. "You buy."

"That figures," she said. "Lead on."

So he led on, aware of the Busters on his flanks, watching him like carnivorous sheepdogs, knowing Jeffords also lurked somewhere in the vicinity, and they went to the open-fronted coffee shop that the Busters had already checked out, to be sure there was no back exit. They sat at an empty table in the front row, just off the pedestrian area, which was also part of the deal. While waiting to be waited on, Meehan said, "You had no trouble. Flights and all."

"All I know is," she said, "I got a call at the MCC this morning, five minutes after I arrived, hadn't even seen my first client yet, I'm told to forget my caseload for today, other people are taking over, I'm to go home and pack for a trip, certainly overnight, maybe longer, a Mr. Eldridge will come pick me up at ten-thirty." She gave him a suspicious look. "Who's this guy Eldridge?"

"Never heard of him."

"Really? Very strange guy," she told him. "Nervous, skinny, young, talked all the time, didn't say a single solitary useful thing."

A very very old waitress arrived then, to ask them what they wanted, and turned out their desires were modest: black coffee for him, a diet decaf cappuccino for her. The waitress tottered away, and Meehan said, "What the hell's a diet decaf cappuccino?"

"A state of mind," she said. "Tell me what's going on."

"Well," he said, "there's a presidential election coming up, pretty soon."

"Stop right there," she told him. "I'm forty-one years old, I don't have the life expectancy for this."

"It's short," he promised. "The people working to help the guy get reelected, they found out there's an October Surprise coming up— You've heard of October Surprises."

"Everybody's heard of October Surprises," she assured him.

Not bothering to correct her, he said, "They want to stop this October Surprise, and to do it they need a burglary, and—"

"Oh, my God," she said. "Watergate? Don't they *ever* learn?"

"Well, yeah, they learn," Meehan told her. "This time, they learned they oughta get a pro—"

"So they look in prison," she said sardonically.

"Go ahead, have your cheap joke," he said. "The fact is I'm pretty good at what I do."

"Usually, maybe."

"Nobody's good *all* the time," he said.

"In your business," she told him, "you have to be."

"Well, that's true. Anyway, they get access to federal things, like the MCC, and some Parks Department place they've kept me in since then, and they want me to go get this October Surprise for them."

"And what am *I* supposed to do?" she demanded. "Start preparing your insanity defense?"

"I told them I wanted you," he explained. "These people are politicians, I don't trust them, they make me uncomfortable."

"Well, your instincts are good, anyway," she said.

"So we're negotiating," he went on, "and I felt I didn't want to be alone in the room, and you're the only lawyer I know, so I said, get me Elaine Goldfarb or there's no deal, and they said okay."

"Well, whoever they are," she said, "they've got clout. They got you out of the MCC, and they got me. But what am I supposed to *do?*"

"Watch my back. Isn't that what lawyers do?"

"In a way," she said, then frowned at him. "But you're still in serious trouble with the law," she pointed out. "I'm surprised you didn't just tell these people, sure, no problem, then run for the hills."

"They've got two sturdy ex-cops bird-dogging me," Meehan told her. "Unfortunately, I'm not running anywhere."

The waitress returned, bowed beneath the weight of their coffees and the check, in a big leatherette book. She distributed all, faded away, and Elaine Goldfarb said, "I see one of them, over there. Oh, and there's the other one." She frowned, which created unfortunate gray vertical lines between her thick black eyebrows. "Who's the one lurking over there?"

"A politician," Meehan told her. "Named Jeffords. He's the one got me out of the MCC."

"I'm surprised they let *him* out," she commented, and sipped cappuccino. "So what happens now?"

"You got luggage?"

"Of course I've got luggage. What do you think I am, a Camp Fire girl?"

"Okay, fine," he said. "If you agree to be my lawyer, we call oley oley infree, collect everybody, collect your luggage, and go back to the Outer Banks."

"The Outer Banks!" She reared back to look him up and down. "You get around more than the average federal prisoner, I'll give you that," she said.

## 15

SHE HAD TWO bags, and they were both heavy, even the one on wheels; especially the one on wheels, because the wheels were stuck. She stood next to the revolving luggage carousel, with its endless variety of parcels, far more various than the passengers waiting for them, and silently looked at Meehan, both bags at her feet. He hefted one, then the other, then looked around for a Buster. Catching one's eye—who did not want that eye caught—he gestured for the guy to come over, and when he did, glowering in Meehan's face as a way not to acknowledge the presence of Elaine Goldfarb, Meehan said, "These things are very heavy." The Buster continued to look at him, so Meehan expounded: "If you and your pal shlep them, I won't run away."

The Buster looked at the bags, and back at Meehan: "And if we won't?"

"We'll see who wins the marathon."

Disgusted, the Buster gave the other Buster a wave, and when number two arrived he explained the situation in quick irritated fashion.

"Fuck it," said number two. "No big deal."

So each Buster carried a bag, followed by Meehan and
Elaine Goldfarb, out of the baggage area and the terminal and
through the sunshine toward their car. Midway, Jeffords caught
up, hissing, "That is not in their job profile."

"Mine neither," Meehan said. "Elaine Goldfarb, may I present Pat Jeffords? He played you yesterday."

"I wondered what happened yesterday," she said.

Jeffords made a face. "A lot happened yesterday," he said.
"And I'm beginning to think it isn't over yet."

The next question concerned seating in the car. Jeffords
wanted to sit in back with Meehan and his lawyer, but Meehan
said, "We're gonna have an attorney-client discussion back
here. Ride up front with the muscle."

Elaine Goldfarb said, "If we're operating here anywhere
within the shadow of the umbrella of the law, my client is right.
He and I have to talk, and I take it you don't have two cars, or
a nearby conference room."

"There isn't enough space up front," Jeffords complained.

Meehan looked, and it was a bench seat up there, not
buckets, so nobody would have to sit on anybody's lap.
"Plenty of room," he said.

Meanwhile, the Busters had stashed the luggage in the
trunk and were waiting around to see what next. Exasperated,
Jeffords said, "Very well. I sit by the window."

So they did; the Busters and Jeffords presenting a solid wall
of shoulder, slightly crumpled together, up front, while Meehan
and Elaine Goldfarb luxuriated in all the room in the back seat.
They remained silent back there awhile, he looking out at the
scenery, wondering what he was doing here, wondering what
the alternatives were, wondering why the only known alternative in the world was the MCC, while beside him she had taken
out of the big saggy black leather shoulderbag she carried in
addition to those two heavy suitcases a ballpoint pen and a

small pad, in which she took the occasional note, meantime chewing the wrong end of the pen.

Once they were on the interstate, she leaned closer to him to say, "You're gonna have to tell me about this October Surprise."

"All I know is—"

"Hold on," she said, and leaned forward to where Jeffords had turned into one giant ear, straining toward them. Tapping the wet end of her ballpoint against the shoulder under that ear, she said, "Turn on the radio."

The look he swiveled to give them was almost innocent: "Sure. What kind of music do you like?"

"Music you can't hear over," she said.

He gave her a very-funny grimace, but leaned forward, displacing all those shoulders, to switch on the radio. Soon, nasal laments of untrustworthy lovers met in bars filled the car with the sorrows of trying to get through life while unutterably stupid, and Elaine Goldfarb leaned close again, to murmur beneath the anguish, "Go ahead."

"They say it's a package of bad evidence that could hurt the president," he told her. "A videotaped confession, and supporting documents. They wouldn't say what the topic was."

"Videotaped confession." She pursed her lips. "It's no traffic ticket."

"I don't think so, no. And Jeffords and these people are part of something called CC."

"Oh, sure," she said. "The Campaign Committee."

"Whatever that is."

"The campaign apparatus for the president. All his speech writers, planners, travel organizers, advance men, spokespeople, the whole crowd that goes to make up a campaign. And sometimes, like now," she said, "the campaign has to do something a little off the books."

"This is a little off the table completely," Meehan suggested.

"Sure, but it's the problem they've got. And, given the circumstances, they're smart to come to you."

"They said 'outsource.'"

She grinned. "That's right, you're an outsource. So your job is just to go where this package is hidden, and get it, and bring it back."

"Right."

"Well, that's fine," she said. "What you're doing is technically illegal, but it isn't a major felony, so I think we can—" She peered at him. "Am I missing something?"

"Um," he said.

She pointed the glistening pen-end at him. "I am an officer of the court," she told him. "Do not tell me if you plan to commit anything *really* illegal."

"Count on it," Meehan said.

# 16

THIS TIME, THERE was no problem getting through the gate. Pointing at the sign, Meehan said, "NPS?"

"National Park Service," she said.

"Ah." So this CC wasn't exactly government, but it could use government stuff. Not bad.

When they got out at the same building as before, there was a brief pause while the Busters got the luggage from the trunk, during which Meehan managed to sidle close to Jeffords and, from the corner of his mouth, mutter, "We don't need to talk about antiques."

Jeffords gave him a surprised smirk. "Wheels within wheels," he said.

"Whatever."

They went into the building, and while the Busters stomped upstairs with the bags Jeffords led the way down to the big office at the end of the hall where Meehan had had breakfast with Benjamin, who was there again, standing from the desk as they entered, smiling his avuncular stockbroker smile, saying, "Ah, all went well."

"So far," Jeffords said.

Benjamin came around the desk toward Elaine Goldfarb, hand out: "Bruce Benjamin."

"Elaine Goldfarb."

"And you have agreed to represent this scalawag. Very warmhearted of you."

"But softheaded, you mean," she said, returning his smile and his hand.

"Not at all."

Meehan said, "She gets paid."

"Well, of course," Benjamin said, and Jeffords said, "By the State of New York, isn't it?"

"By your CC," Meehan told him. "You were gonna get me a lawyer from Washington, right? Who was gonna pay *him?*"

Benjamin said, "Yes, Francis, I take your point. Ms. Goldfarb, we will certainly pay you for your time in this matter."

Meehan said, "The lawyer from Washington; how much would he have charged?"

Jeffords, outraged, said, "Oh, *really!*"

Laughing, Elaine Goldfarb said to Benjamin, "Apparently, Meehan and I represent each other."

"So it would seem," Benjamin said. Jeffords was the excitable one, but Benjamin remained calm.

Meehan said, "How much?"

Benjamin gestured to Elaine Goldfarb. "I defer to you."

"Well," she said, "if they brought in a lawyer from Washington on this, he'd certainly charge three hundred dollars an hour, probably more."

"Agreed," Benjamin said. "Shall we say a retainer for twenty hours?"

"Sounds good," she said.

"Give me your Social Security number and so on when we finish here," Benjamin told her, "and I'll have a check cut for you. Now, if we could sit and get to the topic at hand."

So they sat, where they'd had breakfast, and Jeffords said

to Benjamin, "We don't have to worry about any antiques here, just what we want from Francis."

"Understood," Benjamin said.

Elaine Goldfarb looked brightly around at everybody. Meehan told her, "Don't worry about it, it's nothing."

"Fine," she said. She had her yellow pad and ballpoint pen out of her leather bag; holding both, she said to Benjamin, "From what Meehan told me on the way down, you have a certain sensitive object you want him to retrieve for you, in return for which you propose to make his current legal problems go away."

"Exactly," Benjamin said.

"How?"

Benjamin nodded. "Fair question. We can do it one of three ways. The records can simply disappear—"

"Too many," she said, shaking her head, making a note, "in too many places."

"You may be right. Option two is to proceed to trial, making the evidence disappear and guaranteeing dismissal. This would of course require a return to custody."

"The MCC," Meehan said.

"Afraid so."

Elaine Goldfarb said, "And number three?"

"Witness protection program, new identity, transfer to Arizona or some such."

Meehan said, "Out of the MCC and into the frying pan. I'm a New Yorker."

Elaine Goldfarb said, "It doesn't seem to me you have an adequate procedure to make good on your representations to my client."

"Make a suggestion," Benjamin offered.

"A presidential pardon."

Jeffords began to bob around, saying, "No no no, that would raise far too many questions."

"I'm afraid Pat's right," Benjamin said, looking sad.

"Then a governor's pardon, State of New York."

"Similar problem."

Everybody was stuck. Meehan saw it and heard the silence and, remembering a stunt he'd heard about, a friend of a friend, in a different context, used it to get out from under a falling safe, said, "Switch it to juvenile court."

They all looked at him. Jeffords said, "For one thing, your voice has changed."

"I bet you could do it," Meehan said. "It's all in the bureaucracy, right? Switch me to juvenile court, closed session, I plead guilty, time served."

Elaine Goldfarb said, "Which is how long?"

"If we count today," Meehan said, "twelve days."

Jeffords said, "Why would we count today?"

Meehan looked at him. "What am I, free to go?"

Elaine Goldfarb said to Benjamin, "What have you done about the paperwork at this point, his whereabouts?"

"Pat knows that," Benjamin said, and Jeffords said, "The MCC thinks he's in Otisville, and Otisville thinks he's in the MCC."

"So he's still serving time," she said. "And if you could transfer his case to juvenile court, to a judge who wouldn't make difficulties, he could first release Meehan into my custody, I undertake to assure his presence at a hearing in chambers, probably early next week, he pleads guilty, he's remanded into my custody again in lieu of parole, and we could very easily make the paperwork look kosher." Smiling at Meehan, she said, "Good thinking."

"Already," Meehan said, "I feel like a kid again."

# 17

MEEHAN AWOKE WITH a smile on his lips. He didn't even mind the *bzzt-bzzt* of the phone, nor the chirpy voice telling him it was oh eight hundred hours. Life, which only two days ago had looked like a horror story, in which the MCC had only been the preview to someplace even worse, like Leavenworth, now seemed sweet.

Elaine Goldfarb had come through like a champ. She was going to get him out from under that lousy federal hijacking rap, she was making it possible for him to return to the world a free man, and she'd even managed to negotiate him a thousand bucks in walking-around money, which he was to receive in cash this very morning, when they would leave for the flight back from Norfolk to LaGuardia, in New York City. All he'd have to do then, other than keep an appointment some time soon in juvenile court, was put together a string of guys he knew—he was already thinking of some likely possibilities—and go visit an antique firearms collection. Jeffords had given him phone numbers so he could arrange to drop off the incriminating package once he got hold of it, and then he was completely and totally out from under. Not bad.

Humming, which he did badly because he had very little practice at it, Meehan got out of bed and went over to raise the venetian blind and look out at a sunny day. Of course it was a sunny day, they were all going to be sunny days from now on. Soon he would shower and have his breakfast and be on his way, loose as a goose.

Gazing out at the clipped lawns of this Park Service enclave, little people in olive drab uniforms moving this way and that like an animated model for the real thing, Meehan made himself slow down, slow down, and forced himself to think. Didn't one of the ten thousand rules cover this situation?

Yeah; don't count your chickens.

After breakfast in the cafeteria, Jeffords took Meehan away for what he called a "briefing," telling Elaine Goldfarb, "We'll just be a few minutes, and then we'll head for the airport."

"Fine," she said. "I'll have another coffee."

Bruce Benjamin wasn't around today, so it was just Jeffords and Meehan in the seating segment of the big office, where Jeffords produced a road map of Massachusetts, a small notepad, and a pen. Giving all these of Meehan, he said, "You should write it down, so it's just your handwriting."

"Right."

"The man's name is Burnstone."

"I knew that," Meehan said.

"You don't know his first name, or his address."

"Fine." Meehan poised pen over pad.

Jeffords said, "His name is Clendon Burnstone the Fourth."

"Uh-huh."

"The address is Burnstone Trail, Ashley Falls."

Meehan looked at, but didn't unfold the map. "Where's Ashley Falls?"

"Southwest corner of the state, near both Connecticut and New York. Burnstone doesn't actually live *in* Ashley Falls, but on an estate near it." Taking a folded slip of paper from his shirt pocket, he read, "Route Seven-A north, left on Spring Road, left on Burnstone Trail."

Meehan wrote, then stopped. "That's it? No pictures of the house, floor layouts?"

"We're leaving that to the professional," Jeffords said.

Only one Buster drove this time, Jeffords up front with him. Now that the deal was set, Jeffords was calmer, more easygoing. "You've been an interesting guy to know, Francis," he said, as they drove north, and to Elaine Goldfarb he said, "Have him tell you how he saw through me right away, right from the very first second, at the MCC, when I said I was his new lawyer and he said no, you're not. No, he didn't say it, he *wrote it down.* Have him tell you about it on the plane."

"I will," she said.

At the terminal, it turned out Jeffords was physically incapable of even *seeing* heavy pieces of luggage, so what it came down to was, the remaining Buster carried one of the monster suitcases and Meehan hauled the other, along with his own modest ditty bag.

At security, Jeffords slipped a thick legal-size envelope into Meehan's hand, which Meehan slipped under his shirt, and Jeffords said, "If we have the package in hand by Thursday, all well and good. If not, you become an escaped prisoner, a fugitive, probably armed and dangerous, shoot on sight."

"Thanks," Meehan said, and Jeffords and the Buster marched off.

Meehan turned to see Elaine Goldfarb giving him a mildly surprised look: "You're still here."

"Well, sure," he said.

"I bet myself, two-to-one odds, you'd take off the second those guys were out of sight. Or is it the New York flight you want, get back on home turf?"

"Ms. Goldfarb, I'm not running away," Meehan said. "Why would I run away? All I do is get this little package for these people and my legal problems go right out the window."

"The preschool window."

"Whatever window works," Meehan said.

She was dissatisfied. "I've read your history," she said. "Why would you stick around if there's no profit in it for you?"

He knew how to look guiltless when necessary: meeting her gaze eye for eye, he said, "Getting a clean slate is profit enough for me."

"Uh-huh," she said. "Since you're actually coming along, let's get on the plane."

Traveling north, over the battlefields of Pennsylvania, she gave him her home address and phone number, saying, "I work out of my apartment," which is another way to say she didn't have an office. She seemed to him pretty sharp, so he wondered what she was doing in this bottom-feeder job. Some of them did it because they were dedicated to truth, justice, and the American way, and those were the ones you had trouble meeting their eyes. Some had the bottom-feeder jobs because they were bottom-feeders. But some, in Meehan's experience, drifted into these positions because they were contrarians; sooner or later, they stopped getting along with everybody. He wondered if Elaine Goldfarb was one of those.

While he was wondering, she was talking: "When I get to my place, I'll start making the calls. According to Bruce B, the transfer to juvenile court should be taking place this morning, so I just have to find the right venue and the right judge."

"What right venue?"

"Well, the judge we want might not be in Manhattan," she explained. "In fact, it might be easier all around to move the case to another borough."

That was one of the great things about the law; they

couldn't help but make it too complicated, so that in the nooks
and crannies an actual person might live.

She was going on: "Once I make an appointment, I'll give
you a call. Where do I reach you?"

"Well, I don't know," he said. "Where I was staying before
was just temporary, and I been gone awhile, and the cops
came there after my arrest to pick up my stuff, so I think maybe
I don't live there any more. I'll have to find a place."

She gave him a funny look. "You mean the stuff in that little carry-on bag of yours is everything you own in the world?"

"Sure," he said. He didn't see any point mentioning the little cash stashes he had salted away here and there, figuring
everybody has such things so she'd take it for granted. And
come to think of it, a couple of those older stashes he ought
to deal with, now that the goddam government was changing
all the money.

Government; everywhere you turn.

She couldn't get over the skimpiness of his worldly goods.
"Maybe you ought to rethink crime as a career path," she said.

"I do, all the time," he said, "but nothing else gives me the
same job satisfaction."

She decided to let that go, saying, "All right. When you get
settled, call me. If I'm not there, leave a number where I can
reach you."

"Sure," he said. "Listen, did Jeffords tell you about the deadline on this thing?"

She raised an eyebrow. "Deadline? I know they don't have
much time, if they're trying to avoid an October Surprise."

"Next Thursday," he told her. "Either I get them the package by then, or it goes public I'm an escaped prisoner, armed
and dangerous, every cop in the world memorizing my mug
shot."

Outraged, she said, "That should have been part of the ne-
gotiation! They can't speak to my principal behind my back!"

"Well, they did," Meehan said. "Jeffords did. And they got a legit time problem, I can't argue that. So if you could stall this court thing, it would be better. I'm gonna be busy the next few days."

"No details," she said.

# 18

No GREAT DISTANCE from New York City's Port Authority bus
terminal on Eighth Avenue in Manhattan (which the locals call
the "port of authority"), there are a number of blocky, six-to-
eight-story hotel-motels that don't at all mind customers who
pay cash and don't have a lot of luggage and didn't arrive in
their own automobile. In a fourth-floor room of one of these,
Meehan unpacked his ditty bag, ignored his view out through
several lumpy grimy factory buildings and warehouses in the
general direction of the Hudson River and New Jersey, neither
of which was quite visible from here, and sat cross-legged on
the bed with the phone between his shins and a sheet of the
motel's stationery atop a Yellow Pages by his right knee. Holding the motel's ballpoint pen in his right hand, he squinted at
the opposite wall and his own history, looking for a crew.
From time to time, he wrote a set of initials on the stationery.
Initials was as far as he was prepared to commit these people
to writing, and also the initials were reversed.

Forty minutes of cogitation produced eleven sets of initials,
which with luck might render down to the three guys he felt
he'd probably need to come along on this trip. One guy to

drive, one guy to do the heavy lifting—the older the firearm, he suspected, the heavier—and one guy to romance the locks. Meehan himself was the general, the mastermind, the guy who pulled it all together. Sort of like a movie producer. So now was the time to start trying to make contact with these guys.

Working within the strictures of the ten thousand rules, there were a number of taboos concerning the telephone. You had to use it, because you couldn't physically travel to every place where everybody was, but on the other hand you couldn't really say anything on it. So the phone was necessary in order to make contact, but useless for communication.

However, within the general rule that you never write anything down, you *certainly* never write down any phone numbers, so in addition to the telephone having this severely limited usefulness it was also necessary to memorize all these phone numbers, in which at any moment the first three digits might change, due to seismic upheavals in the ether-world of area codes.

Sometimes Meehan found himself thinking that, if the Pony Express was still up and running, he'd be a customer.

So here's the drill. First he looks at a set of initials, then he reverses them, then he remembers who he had in mind when he put the initials down, then he racks his brain for that guy's last known phone number, and then he dials it.

*"The number you have dialed is no longer in service. The num—"*

Cross off a set of initials, repeat process for next set.

"Hom yang."

"Uhh, is Mikey there?"

"Fring mititako hoolak?"

"Mikey. I'm looking for Mikey."

"Fleetferop! Miggle kaba fucking pibblesak? Fuck no!"

"Sorry."

And repeat.

"Hello." Tired female voice.

Meehan took another look at the initials, reversed them, said, "Hi, I'm looking for Bert."

"So am I, brother," she said.

"Oh."

"You got any other places to try?"

"No, this is the only number I—"

"You cocksuckers all cover up for him, don'tcha? All stick together. Let me tell you—"

Even after he'd hung up, the phone seemed to continue to vibrate for another few seconds. Meehan gave it a reproachful look.

Three out of eleven, gone already. It was true that the kind of people he tended to know did not make a habit of staying in one place very long, but this was getting ridiculous. He was almost afraid of the next set of initials. Who knew what might have happened to Woody in the last four months?

Then it occurred to him he was supposed to call whatser-name. Ms. Goldfarb, the lawyer. Here was her phone number, completely written out with her name and address and everything, on a piece of paper in his shirt pocket. So probably the thing to do was take a break from calling up old chums, even though he was feeling the pressure of next Thursday's dead-line, and call Goldfarb instead, give her the phone number at the motel here.

So Meehan dialed the number on the piece of paper, and on the third ring it was answered by a very gruff male voice, saying, "Goldfarb residence."

"Elaine Goldfarb, please." Who was this guy? Was Goldfarb married?

"She's not available right now," said the gruff voice, clearly trying to make itself less gruff, more telephone-friendly. "Could I take a message?"

"Yeah, I'm supposed to give her a contact phone number," Meehan said. "How to reach me."

"Sure, I'll take that."

"Okay, my name's Meehan, my—"

"Oh, Meehan!" the guy said, very pleased. "Yeah, she wants to talk to you!"

"I thought she wasn't available."

"She isn't here right this *second*, but she wants to see you. I think she said it was urgent."

"Oh, yeah?"

"You got the address here, don't you?"

On the same slip of paper. Meehan looked at it, squinting, thinking. "Yeah, I got it. Two-seventy-nine West End, apartment eight-H."

"That's the place," the guy said. "Come straight over here, she wants to see you urgent. Okay? Come right now."

"Right," Meehan said, and hung up, and sniffed the air.

What is wrong with this picture?

# 19

TWO-HUNDRED-SEVENTY-NINE West End was a big old stone apartment building in the Eighties, half a block wide, with an awning above the front door and a doorman inside it. Meehan had walked up from his new residence, maybe a mile and a half, pausing at a hardware store along the way to make a few innocent purchases that fit nicely in his pockets. He walked by the facade of 279 with hardly a glance at the doorman, who stood in his uniform of navy blue trimmed with gold behind the glass of the entryway, gazing outward, hands folded at his crotch, waiting for somebody to arrive in or want a taxicab.

At the corner, Meehan turned left, to walk next to the side of the building and to see that the service entrance was an eight-foot-high iron gate, shut tight, with a garbage-can-lined alleyway running ten feet deep behind it, burrowing into the building, with a closed metal door at the far end. Ahead of him was Riverside Drive, and beyond that the Hudson River and America.

Meehan circled the block, thinking. The only way in was past the doorman, but he didn't want to be announced. Coming back around to West End, he crossed it and continued on to Broadway, turning south there until he found the second hardware store of the day. In this one, he bought a four-foot metal ladder and a smoke detector, then walked back to 279 with the ladder's next-to-last rung resting on his right shoulder, smoke detector in his left hand. This time, he walked straight to the building, where the doorman, faintly surprised, opened the door and said, "Yeah?"

"Smoke detector," Meehan told him, showing it.

The doorman looked at the box. "For what?"

"Elevator."

"The elevator? Nobody told *me*."

"Well, they told me, replace the smoke detector."

"Which elevator?" the doorman demanded.

"In the back."

Sounding dubious, the doorman said, "Go ahead. They didn't tell me a thing about it."

"Thanks, pal," Meehan said, and carried the ladder past the elevator at the front end of the lobby because he was operating from the assumption that they would number the apartments from the front, which would put H at the back.

The elevator was already here. Meehan boarded, didn't look back to see if the doorman was watching him, opened the ladder, started up it, and the elevator door closed. He immediately pushed 8.

Having no further need for the ladder, he closed it and left it leaning in the elevator. In the short hall here, he looked at the apartment doors, and found H first on the right. He approached it, reaching into his pockets for some of his recent purchases, but there was something weird about the door. A length of shiny electrician's tape was stretched over the striker plate, from the outside of the jamb inward, so that when the door was closed the bolt wouldn't snap into place. The door would close, but it wouldn't lock.

Who would do a thing like that? Who would put a piece of

tape over a doorlock that you could see from outside? Nobody Meehan knew.

Very cautiously, he pushed open the door. What he looked in at was a small square vestibule with heavy woodwork around the door frames, painted thirty times the last hundred years. A Utrillo print hung on the wall to the left, over a rickety little table with an empty cut-glass vase on it. To the right was a closed door, probably a closet. Ahead was a doorless entryway to a living room furnished out of the Salvation Army; heavy old pieces, kind of shabby but more or less kept up.

Meehan slid through the doorway and let the door slowly close behind him, having to hold it because there was a very strong spring in the hinges. Maybe that's why the tape was on there; the unlocking button was stuck, as they often were in these old buildings because nobody ever used them, and the door simply wouldn't stay open by itself. But why would anybody want it to stay open?

The door closed gently enough, but nevertheless something in its mechanism, at the last second, went *click*. Meehan froze, and his alert ears heard a chair scrape on a floor, two rooms away.

No. He pulled open the door on his right, and it not only was the closet he'd expected, it was full of coats and sweaters and scarves and overshoes. Meehan slid in, pulling the door shut behind himself, scrunching through all the hanging coats, getting behind them, standing with shoulder blades against the inner wall, face in a lot of wool shoulders.

"Yehudi?" It sounded like the same gruff voice Meehan had heard on the phone. Now it was in the living room, headed this way. "Yehudi?"

Pause. Do I want to sneeze, Meehan wondered, and decided no, he didn't. That was a relief.

The closet door opened. Meehan didn't move a corpuscle. The closet door closed.

Meehan waited a good long time, what seemed like hours but was probably forty seconds, then very slowly and quietly pushed the closet door open. Nobody in the vestibule. Unfortunately, the door opened toward the living room, so he had to keep opening it until he could lean out and see around it, but then fortunately the living room was empty. He took a step from the closet, and the hall door to his left pushed open toward him, and Meehan teleported himself back into the closed closet, shoulder blades against the inner wall.

Somebody in the vestibule. A nearby voice called, "Mostafa?" Then the closet door opened, and Meehan stopped breathing.

"*There* you are," said the original gruff voice, from some distance away.

The new one—must be Yehudi—pawed around in the closet looking for a hanger while Meehan's cheekbones shriveled, then found one, as he said, "I got here as soon as I could. I take it he didn't show up yet."

"No. The doorman will have to announce him. And who knows where he's coming from?"

Listening to them now, this close, it seemed to Meehan they both had faint accents, maybe the same, maybe not.

Yehudi shoved the hanger back into the closet, now with a zippered vinyl jacket on it, and said, "Do we need a ladder? There's one in the elevator."

"For what? No, leave it."

"What I'd really like right now," Yehudi said, "is a glass of tea."

"I have some brewed," Mostafa told him. "Oh, take that tape off the door, now you're back."

"Right." Yehudi laughed. "Wouldn't look good if our boy noticed *that*, would it?"

They went away then, chuckling together. Meehan waited until he couldn't stand the silence any more, then moved forward through the coats, reaching for the door, feeling something hard and heavy in the inner pocket of the vinyl jacket Yehudi had just parked here. Knowing what it was, but having to verify the knowledge anyway, he felt around to the opening of the jacket, reached inside, and stuck fingers down into the pocket. It was pitch black in here, but his fingers knew a gun when they felt one; a small flat automatic. Afraid he might accidentally touch the trigger and shoot himself in the chest, he slowly inched his fingers back outa there.

Who were these people? Foreign, and violent, or at least armed. Meehan thought Yehudi was a Jewish name. Was Mostafa?

And what should he do about them? He himself was not a violent person, never had been. Sometimes, on a job, it would be a good idea for somebody to carry heat, but that somebody was never Meehan, and he preferred it when the heat remained implicit. So he wasn't going to lay hold of Yehudi's automatic now, brace the two guys over their glasses of tea, and demand to know what was going on around here.

Still, he wanted to know. Today was Friday, October 15, and he had only until next Thursday, October 21, to put together a crew, case the Burnstone gun collection, plot and execute the job, and deliver the package to Jeffords. Not much time, and he didn't want to spend great stretches of it hanging around in Goldfarb's closet.

So it was time to get out of here, figure out the situation, find out if he was going to need a new lawyer; for instance, if Goldfarb was lying dead in the bedroom, certainly a possibility. That happy thought having given him a slightly queasy feeling, he swallowed noisily, then silently pushed open the closet door.

Voices, probably two rooms away. Casual, chatting voices. Meehan eased out of the closet and through the vestibule into the living room, wanting to be close enough to hear what they were saying but not close enough to be part of the conversation.

In the living room, there were two windows on the left, a closed door on the right, and an open door straight ahead through which he could see part of a kitchen. It was from the kitchen the voices came. Meehan took a step toward that door, and the closed door on the right opened. He froze, and Goldfarb came out, looking angry and determined. The first thing he noticed was the set of handcuffs dangling from her left wrist, and the second thing he noticed was the pistol in her right hand. *Another* gun! Were all these people crazy?

Apparently. Goldfarb, determined on what she was doing, not noticing Meehan in the doorway to her left, turned toward the open kitchen doorway to her right, snub-nosed pistol held out in front of her.

No! You don't want to do that. "Sss," Meehan said, and again, "Sss!"

Startled, she turned her head, then looked absolutely astonished to see him there. He made come-to-me gestures with both hands, like the navy man on the aircraft carrier guiding the airplane into position. He backed into the vestibule, gesturing and shaking his head. Do not go into the kitchen. Do not go among those people in the kitchen.

She hesitated. He could feel the intensity with which she wanted a confrontation, but a wiser head was going to prevail, and at this particular moment he was the wiser head around here, so he gestured more vigorously than ever, then mouthed NO, then turned both hands into guns and pantomimed them shooting at each other. He clutched his chest over his heart and let his head loll, tongue hanging out. Then he reached behind him for the knob of the apartment door, turned it slowly and quietly, and pulled the door open. Next he backed through the doorway to the hall, holding the door with right hand, beckoning with left, and all at once she made her decision. She held her cuffed hand up, palm out: wait.

Okay, he'll wait. She turned and hurried back into the room she'd come out of, and when she returned ten long seconds later the gun was replaced by that big black leather bag, bumping on her hip. She hurried toward him, and he let the door snick shut behind her.

Immediately, she had a cellphone out of her bag. "Wait," he whispered. "Who you calling?"

"The cops!"

"Don't. Come away from the door. Tell me what's going on."

She let him move her down the hall to the elevator as she said, "I don't *know* what's going on. They're spies or something. They want to know about *you*."

"Me? What about me?"

"They want to know what you're supposed to get for the president."

He stared at her. "They *know* about that?"

"They don't know what it is, that's what they came around for, but I don't know either, so they were waiting around to make contact with you."

"And you're gonna call the cops? Ms. Goldfarb, let's take a ride in an elevator," he finished, having already buttoned for it and it now arriving.

She didn't want to board. "I can't leave those people in my apartment!"

"I can't think of a better place for them," he said. "Who we want to call is Jeffords. If you call the cops, what do you tell them?"

"I don't, I—"

"Elevator," he insisted, being tired of holding its door open, and at last she stepped aboard. He followed her, and pushed LOBBY.

She was looking at the ladder. "Where'd that come from?"

"I brought it," he said. "When we go out past your door-man, we're not together. Then we'll go over to Broadway and take a cab down to my place."

The look she gave him was ready to turn very hostile. "Your place?"

"That's where Jeffords' phone number is. Listen, Ms. Gold-farb, they got you scared and they got you mad, but now it's time to slow down and think like a lawyer. You've got foreign spies that *know* there's something bad out there about your president, but they don't know what it is, but they'd like to get it for themselves. Why not have their own handle on the American president's back? But where did they find out the part they already know? Only from Jeffords' organization, that campaign committee. So he's who we want to talk to, because with the cops, you get one sentence in, *then* what you gonna say?"

The elevator stopped and the door opened. Picking up his ladder, "After you," Meehan said.

# 20

Their cabby, running down Broadway, wore a skinny headset-mike thing so he could keep both hands on the wheel while engaged in a passionate, sometimes angry, sometimes sorrowful, telephone call in his native Dzavhan-Mongol dialect, a language that sounds mostly like a water buffalo clearing its throat. Under cover of this monologue, Goldfarb brought Meehan up to date.

The doorman had announced the intruders as being from Bruce Benjamin. Not seeing any reason for anybody to lie about that, she'd said okay, send them up. When she opened the apartment door to them, they promptly pulled guns on her and handcuffed her with the cuff chain going around the cold water pipe under her bathroom sink. With her in that awkward and uncomfortable position, they made threats, but didn't touch her, insisting she tell them what it was Meehan was supposed to steal for the president. When she convinced them she didn't know the answer to that question, because why would anybody have given her that information, they decided to stick around until Meehan should make contact with his attorney, then ask *him*. Very angry, she had spent a long time spitting

PUT A LID ON IT

on her right wrist—"You were spitting mad," he said, which left her unamused—and trying to squeeze that cuff off. When she finally succeeded, having scraped the skin pretty badly—"Ouch," he said, looking at it, "we better get you some first-aid stuff." "Later," she said—she immediately got her own firearm from her bedside table drawer, being too mad even to think about her cellphone, which was probably just as well, and marched out of her bedroom to find Meehan himself there, having been very brave and unexpectedly altruistic, racing up there to rescue her.

Meehan didn't mind that. If she wanted to believe he'd gone to her place on a mission of mercy, and not merely to find out what the situation meant for his own personal well-being, that was fine with him. "It was nothing," he said, and watched while she paid the cab.

In the motel lobby, he said, "They got a little gift shop, maybe you can find something to put on your wrist, while I go up and get the phone number."

"Why don't I come with you?"

"I'm not gonna call from *there*," he said, "through the switchboard. We'll find a nice noisy pay phone down by Times Square."

"You're the expert," she said. She had found a rubber band somewhere in her shoulderbag and was using it to hold the dangling part of the handcuff to her left wrist, where it would be less noticeable.

Leaving her to that, he went up to his room and found Jeffords' phone number, and when he came back down to the lobby she had a big square Band-Aid on her right wrist, allegedly flesh-colored, that made her look like a failed suicide. Pointing at it, he said, "Feel any better?"

"I'll feel better when I can go back to an empty apartment," she said.

"Okay, let's find that phone."

The first two outdoor phones they found were broken, quite badly, as though they'd been in use by a person who'd suddenly had a psychotic episode, but the third one was fine. The number Jeffords had given Meehan started with 800, so there was no problem about putting bunches of money in or making the call collect.

Unfortunately, the number also led directly to cheerful inhuman-yet-female voices offering menus. If you want to shit, press 1; if you want to go blind, press 2; that sort of thing. Meehan suffered through this for a very long time, under the keen raptor eye of Goldfarb, twice having to press numbers to lead him to "further options," and then having to be very alert when one of those options was, "Enter the first three letters of your party's name." Squinting at the buttons, Meehan pounded out 5 3 3, leading another voice to say, "If your party is Hal Jeffcott, press one. If your party is Wilma Jefferson, press two. If your party is Patrick Jeffords, press three. If—"

Meehan *whomped* 3. Somewhere a phone began to ring. It rang twice, and then Jeffords' voice, sounding not quite human, said, "Hi, this is Pat Jeffords. I'm sorry I can't take your call right now—"

"Fuck," Meehan commented.

"—please leave your name and number and the time of your call, and I'll get back to you as soon as I can. Have a nice day." Then there was a beep.

"Fuck you, too," Meehan told the recording device. "You know who this is, and the time is—" Aside, to Goldfarb, he said, "What time is it?"

She studied her watch. "Three-forty."

"The time here is three-forty," Meehan recorded, "and I'm standing here at a pay phone on Ninth Avenue in New York City with Goldfarb." He read the number off the face of the machine and said, "You have five minutes to call me back, or the deal is off, and we'll *call* the cops to come get the foreign spies

"Well, Woody," Meehan said, "I'd be happy to give you th whole story over a beer, if I thought you might be interested.

There was a long pause, while the Jell-O hardened, and Meehan had just begun to think Woody would never speak again when he said, "I can listen."

Hearing the suspicion in Woody's voice, Woody wondering if Meehan was a plant the way, in the MCC, Meehan had wondered if Johnson was a plant, Meehan said, "You say where and when."

"You're in the city?"

"Where else?"

"There's a video store on Third between Nineteenth and Twentieth," Woody said. "They keep the porn in the back."

"Sure. What time?"

"Let's see, it's five to four. How about four-thirty? That way we're in and out before the workers stop by on their way home."

Thirty-five minutes to get across town and down. "I'll be there," Meehan said, and abandoned the rest of his list.

The front windows of the video store were spread with posters of kiddy movies. Inside, the store was deep and narrow, lined with video boxes on shelves, more video boxes on carousels down the middle of the place, a bored grandmother seated on a stool behind a counter and cash register next to the door. There were no customers.

The grandmother raised an eyebrow at Meehan but didn't speak, so he didn't either, but walked through to the back, where a closed dark red door with four smallish windows in it bore a sign ADULT. When Meehan opened this door, it chimed, like the Avon lady was coming, or somebody was coming.

But there was nobody in this narrow gaudy back room but Woody, a bony glum-looking black-haired man, looking at his

out of Goldfarb's apartment." Hanging up, he said, "Enough is enough."

"Nicely done," she said. "What if he doesn't call in five minutes?"

"You call the cops, and I steal a car and drive to Idaho."

She said, "Idaho? Why Idaho?"

"Because the feds are afraid to go there," he said, and the phone rang. Picking up the receiver, he said, "Go ahead."

It was Jeffords' voice, gone supersonic: "Spies? Foreign spies? What are you *talking* about?"

"Two guys," Meehan told him, "named Yehudi and Mostafa broke into Goldfarb's apartment. They know you sent me to get something, and they know why, but they don't know what it is. They leaned on Goldfarb, and they wanted to lean on me, but we both got outa there. Let me tell you something, Mr. Jeffords, in my business we don't have leaks, we never have leaks, but in your business you don't have anything *except* leaks, and this one is leaking on *me*. And Goldfarb."

"My God," Jeffords said. "I can't think what, who'd—"

"She wants to go back to her apartment," Meehan interrupted. "Does she call the cops?"

"What? No!"

"So what does she do?"

"I don't— I'll have to look into this."

"In the meantime," Meehan said, "this is distracting me from the job. Remember the deadline?"

"Oh, God."

"You said that before. When can Goldfarb get back into her apartment?"

"I don't know yet, I'll have to check into this."

"Okay, Mr. Jeffords," Meehan said. "Give me a phone number where what I reach is you and not a lot of machines and menus."

"I— Well . . ." Jeffords sighed deeply. "Do you have a pencil?"

"Hold on." To Goldfarb he said, "Can you write this down?"

"Sure." Out of the shoulderbag came pen and notepad.

Meehan told Jeffords, "Say it now," and put the phone by Goldfarb's ear. She wrote down the number, and then Meehan took the phone back, to say, "You're gonna pay to put Goldfarb up in a hotel—"

"Damn," Goldfarb said.

"Of course," Jeffords said.

"—and we'll call you— What is this number you gave me?"

"My cellphone, it's always on my person, not many people have that number."

"Screw up, Mr. Jeffords," Meehan threatened, "and every telemarketer in the *world* is gonna have that number."

"Francis, I've been decent with you—"

"Yeah, yeah. We'll call you in an hour, find out what your progress is."

"Fine. Do that. Fine."

Meehan hung up, and Goldfarb said, "I find I prefer the Goldfarb without the Ms."

"Me, too," Meehan said. "Let's find you a room at my joint."

# 21

GOLDFARB HAD TO go shopping for basics, so Meeha
to his room, looked at his list of reversed initials, an
dered what would turn out to have gone wrong with G

"Hello?"

"Is Woody there?"

Pause: "Do I know that voice?"

"Oh, Woody, harya!" Astonished to find somebody a
home, Meehan said, "I tell you what, I'll go on talking un
remember who I am. One of the ten thousand rules is
work better than eyes."

"Gotcha," Woody said. "But you're inside. Why you c
me from inside?"

"Because I'm outside," Meehan said. "And before
Thursday I gotta do a little stunt that'll not only keep me
side but earn a couple dollars for me and a few friends.
wanna come along?"

Woody had started by sounding phlegmatic; now
sounded as though he were talking through Jell-O: "How c
you're out? You're out? How come?"

watch. "I'm not late," Meehan said, shutting the door (it chimed again), "I'm exactly on time."

"You don't mind," Woody said, "I pat you down."

Moving away from the windowed door, spreading his arms, Meehan said, "This is a weird place to do it."

"Safe sex," Woody said, and patted Meehan here and there, not hard but thorough, looking not for weapons, as Meehan knew, but wires. Done, but looking unsatisfied, he stepped back, folded his arms, and said, "Tell."

"I was in the MCC—"

"On a solid rap," Woody said. "And federal. I heard about it. No way you're out."

"Exactly," Meehan said. "Except, it's federal, and it turns out, there's some people connected to the president, he's running for election, these people are with him, helping—"

"Meehan," Woody said, "what the hell have *you* got to do with the president?"

"They want me to steal something for him," Meehan said. "He's got an evidence problem, just like a normal person, like you or me, and he needs a robber, so they look in the federal cans, they find me, make me the offer. I get this evidence, turn it over, they make my case go away, they can do that. Next week I'm supposed to go to juvenile court, plead guilty, sentenced to time served."

Woody frowned at him. Down inside there, he seemed to be thinking very hard, but not very fast. Finally he said, "How long I known you?"

"Maybe seven, eight years."

"Here's the thing of it," Woody said. "What you just told me there is the rankest bullshit, I wouldn't try that one on my four-year-old nephew, but it's comin outa *you*, and while you contain as much bullshit as anybody it isn't *that* kind of bullshit, not in all the years I known you. It just doesn't have the mark of your kind of invention, and why would you try such bull-

shit on me in the first place? What's in it for you? You aren't trying to entrap me, not with a story like that, you aren't making
me any offers, so what *is* this shit?"

"Well, it's the truth," Meehan said.

"Jesus Christ on a crutch," Woody said. "If it isn't the truth,
what the fuck is it? You can buy me that beer now."

# 22

AT A BOOTH in a dim bar on Third Avenue, beginning to fill up with a mix of office workers and construction workers at the end of their workday, the two of them hunched over Rolling Rocks in the green bottles, Woody listened as Meehan told him the story, from Jeffords' laughable imitation of a lawyer to Meehan's flight back with Goldfarb. He left out the foreign spies because he didn't want to complicate the issue. At the end, he said, "They gave me a G, walking around money. They gave my lawyer a retainer check of six large. These people are Looney Tunes, but they're also serious."

"And you don't know what's in this package," Woody said, "that they want you to get for them."

"I don't want to know," Meehan told him. "I thought it over, and I hear it's a videotaped confession that's got the president worried, do *I* want to know what's on that tape? Do I want the president of the fucking universe worried about *me?*"

"I see what you mean," Woody said. "But if this stuff is just layin around, these people already have their hands on it, how can you be sure you got till next Thursday? Maybe they're gonna spring it tomorrow morning, for the Sunday talk shows."

"The CC people," Meehan said, "seemed to think the October Surprise doesn't happen until later in October. The closer to the election, the more punch it's got."

"Well, that's true. And you talked to Leroy."

"He said if it's Burnstone, and now we know it *is* Burnstone, he wants it."

"Did he say how much is in it?"

"We didn't get into dollars," Meehan said. "I had that CC guy breathing on me. If you want, why not call Leroy yourself? Tell him I asked you to come in with me, ask him how much he thinks we'll make out of it."

Woody considered that idea, drinking beer out of the bottle, then shook his head. "Nah, forget it," he said. "If Leroy's interested, there's gotta be enough in there that I'm interested, too. How big a string, do you think?"

"I was guessing four," Meehan said. "But I gotta see the place first, figure it out. Listen, you doing anything? Whyn't we drive up there tomorrow, give it the double-o?"

"Maybe," Woody said, slowly nodding. All around them, office workers were talking with construction workers, everybody hoping to get lucky. Woody and Meehan, in their own quiet cocoon, contemplated their options. Woody said, "You got a car?"

"No, I got nothing. I was gonna be inside forever, remember?"

"Part of me," Woody said, "is still not getting over this. It's like you got a fairy godmother all at once, or a genie in a lamp." He rubbed the Rolling Rock bottle, closed his eyes, intoned, "I wish I was outa the MCC." He opened his eyes and looked at Meehan. "And here you are."

"So do you want to do it?" Meehan asked him. "Drive up tomorrow?"

"You gonna rent a car?"

"I can't, I don't have any credit cards, they get so antsy

when you try to rent with cash. I figured, I go out to Kennedy, borrow one from long-term parking."

Woody did a click thing with his teeth, suggesting he didn't think much of that idea. He said, "I got a cousin, I can usually borrow the car, I'll give her a call."

"Even better," Meehan agreed.

Woody pulled crumpled paper and a stub of pencil from his pocket. "Where are you?"

"Crowne Royale Motor Home," Meehan told him, "on Ninth." He reeled off the place's phone number, and said, "I'm in room three-eighteen."

"I'll call you in the morning," Woody said. He finished his beer, and at last looked around the bar, saying, "Anybody here we could love?"

# 23

LEAVING WOODY IN conference with a zoftig female construction worker, Meehan went back to the Crowne Royale, room 318, to find the message light blinking on his phone. He retrieved, and heard Goldfarb's recorded voice: "Call me, I'm in five-twenty-three." So he figured out how to dial room-to-room, and she answered right away, saying, "Was the MCC worse than this?"

"You're kidding," he said. "This is heaven."

"I'm dying of boredom here," she said. "I've got nothing around me, none of my books, my food, nothing."

"You've got your own TV and a window and a soft bed and an unlocked door," Meehan told her, "and no bad-smelling felons sharing your space. Be grateful."

"All right, I'm grateful," she said, not sounding it. "I talked with Jeffords."

"Yeah?"

"He's taking the shuttle up, he wants to take us to dinner."

"Instead of solving the problem?"

"We'll ask. Do you have any better clothes?"

"I don't have *any* clothes," he said. "This isn't the life I was gearing up for."

"Good," she said. "Meet me in the lobby."

"Why?"

"You've given me a purpose in life," she said. "I'm gonna dress you."

"Nice jacket," Jeffords said, when they walked up to his table.

The last two hours had been difficult for Meehan. Several of the ten thousand rules had to do with not being the center of attention. Nevertheless, Goldfarb had taken him down to Macy's, which was open late because it was Friday, but where they were somewhat limited in their choices because he couldn't pick out—or, more accurately, *she* couldn't pick out—anything that had to be altered. He needed to buy items he could start using right away.

Still, it worked out. When they left Macy's an hour later, he was carrying two big shopping bags in which were folded two nice pairs of wool slacks, light gray and dark gray, and a nice sports jacket, bluish gray, and two nice dress shirts, white and dark blue, and a nice pair of black shoes with laces, and four pairs of nice black socks. Oh, and a necktie, for God's sake, in maroon and black rectangles.

So here he was, in a hushed midtown restaurant at eight P.M., following a tuxedoed maitre d' to the snowy booth where Jeffords awaited them, and Meehan was in his new duds. Where he'd had choices, he'd gone for light gray and dark blue, and the first thing that happened, even before they sat down, Jeffords complimented him on the jacket. Instead of solving the problem?

"Thanks," Meehan said. "Goldfarb picked it out."

"Well, of course," Jeffords said. "She's your legal adviser."

Goldfarb slid into the booth, Meehan followed, and the

maitre d' bent to ask what they wanted to drink. Goldfarb gave a six-word order in which the only word Meehan understood was "vodka." He looked over at Jeffords and saw in front of him a short thick glass containing ice cubes, a clear liquid, and a little shingle of lime rind. So maybe he wouldn't order a beer after all, but straight rye also didn't seem quite the thing. "I'll have the same as her," he said, and the maitre d' bowed and went away.

"And here we all are," Jeffords said, with a bright look around the table.

Goldfarb cut to the chase: "When can I go home?"

Jeffords beamed at her. "Right after dinner, if you want."

She lit up, sparkling behind those monster eyeglasses. "I can? They're gone?"

"Out of your life," he assured her. "Not out of mine yet, unfortunately, but definitely out of yours."

"What about the hotel room I took?"

"Pay for it, send me the bill, we'll reimburse."

"But I don't have to stay there."

"Not unless you really want to."

"Ha ha," she said.

Meehan said, "Tell me about it."

Jeffords was so goddam bland. "The problem's gone away," he said. "Isn't that enough?"

"Not for me, it isn't," Meehan said. "They were looking for me because they wanted to know what's the maguffin. Well, I don't *know* what's the maguffin, but I know *where's* the maguffin, and they gotta know I know that much, so why won't they come blundering into my caper, leaving electric tape on doors and handcuffing people to sinks?"

"It's dealt with," Jeffords insisted. "Your part is dealt with."

"Tell."

Jeffords sighed, and then was rescued temporarily by a waiter, bringing their drinks. These two were also clear liquid

and ice cubes in short thick glasses, but instead of the page of
lime skin they contained a gold sword-shaped toothpick im-
paling two big green olives. "Ahh," said Goldfarb to her drink,
so Meehan smiled at his, waiting for the waiter to go away.

Which he did, to be immediately followed by another one,
bringing them menus the size of placemats, then hanging
around to tell them tonight's specials, which involved a whole
lot of words to let them know that tonight they could also have
tuna, salmon, or lamb chops. Finally, he went away, and Meehan said, "Tell."

"Wait till we order, Francis," Jeffords said. "Or we'll just be
interrupted a lot."

"Okay, fine."

Goldfarb lifted her glass. "Success," she said.

Jeffords lifted his. "Cheers," he said.

Meehan lifted his, finding it surprisingly heavy. "Evil to our
enemies," he said.

"*I'll* drink to that," Jeffords said, and they all did, Meehan
learning to his surprise that he seemed to have ordered gaso-
line diluted with olive oil.

"You know, Francis," Jeffords said, "it's too bad you didn't
have that nice jacket and tie when we were first traveling together."

"I'm sorry if I was an embarrassment," Meehan said.

"No, that's not what I meant," Jeffords said, and waiter
number two came back to take their order.

Meehan wanted to know why the lamb chops were so special tonight, so that's what he asked for, and when Goldfarb
wanted a nice mesclun salad to start he decided he did, too.

"And the wine list," Jeffords said. "This will only take a
minute," he assured Meehan.

A little longer, not much. Waiter number one came back,
with a leather-bound book, larger than the menus, that looked
as though you should say Mass out of it, and Jeffords paged

through it awhile, the waiter hovering, then said, "I think bin two-seventy-one," and the waiter said, "A very nice choice," and went away.

"Do we have to wait for the tasting," Meehan asked, "and the pouring, and the food arriving, and more water in the water glasses, and the drinks glasses being taken away, and some more wine pouring, and—"

"All right," Jeffords said. "All right, you're right. You remember our first flight down to Norfolk."

"Sure."

"There were two people with us on the plane. Howie Briggs, remember?"

"I remember Cindy better," Meehan said, "but sure."

"Howie Briggs thought you looked a little strange to be on that plane," Jeffords said, "which is why it's unfortunate you weren't dressed then as you are now. When he saw the plane's owner at Hilton Head—"

"Arthur," Meehan said. "Briggs didn't mention a last name."

"Very good," Jeffords said. "Yes, Arthur." His mouth turned down. "Arthur is a very large contributor to the president's campaign," he said, "which gives him close access to much of what we're doing. We now learn— Yes, that's it," he told the wine bottle next to his face, and held one finger up for Meehan to wait.

When next he could speak, he said, "We now learn that Arthur, through various multinational business connections, has, what shall I say, divided loyalties. Conflicts of interest. There are other elements, offshore, about which he feels as strongly as he feels about the reelection of the president. Perhaps more strongly." He looked uncomfortable, fiddled with his wineglass, said, "It seems there's a combined Egyptian-Israeli intelligence task force in this country at the moment, attempting to influence the election. Been here for months. Spending money."

Goldfarb said, "Foreign power brokers always try to horn in on our elections, guarantee themselves a piece of the pie. It's like lobbying."

Jeffords nodded. "Yes, exactly. When Howie Briggs described Francis to Arthur, wondering why such scruffy people should get nice rides on Arthur's private jet, Arthur made inquiries."

"Because you weren't controlling the situation," Meehan said. "As I already pointed out."

"Yes, I know," Jeffords agreed, "you told me so, you're absolutely right. Well, we're learning as we go in this operation."

"Are we," Meehan said.

Jeffords ignored that, saying, "Thank God the people Arthur talked to don't know *what* it is that's out there, but now Arthur's other friends do know something's there. Something exists."

Goldfarb said, "Do they want to get it so they can release it?"

"No," Jeffords said. "They would merely like our president to be deeply in debt to them. Let's say, even more deeply in debt."

Meehan said, "So what happened today, and what's gonna happen tomorrow?"

"After I got your call," Jeffords said, "Bruce and I did some of our own inquiries, and it didn't take long to learn that two or three people had been indiscreet around Arthur." Again he sighed. "It's so hard to maintain security," he told them, "in an organization so full of passionate amateurs and true believers. Some of those people will tell anybody anything, because after all, aren't we all on the same side? Don't we represent beauty and truth?"

"Security breached," Meehan said, dredging that phrase up from some spy novel somewhere. "Now what?"

"Fortunately," Jeffords said, "we do have some hotheads on

call when intimidation is needed, Cuban and Serbian mostly, more recently super-American citizens, and I believe even now"—with a look at his watch—"a few of them are increasing Arthur's cleaning bills, down there at Hilton Head."

"That's not gonna keep—" Meehan stopped and frowned. "Wait a minute. Did you say combined Egyptian and Israeli *intelligence?* I mean, I heard you, but the penny didn't drop. How are you gonna shut *them* down?"

Jeffords said, "We can make it very clear to them, Francis, through various channels, that we know what they know, we know what they were trying to do, and we would be very displeased to hear they were still trying to do it. *Or* let the Other Side know, accidentally or by design, that we know something's up. The only sure way to stop an intelligence operation is to shine a light on it, and that's what you and we have done."

Meehan looked at Goldfarb. "Does that fly?"

"Probably," she said. "Not necessarily."

"Almost guaranteed," Jeffords said.

"Great," Meehan said. "Well, I tell you what, Mr. Jeffords. You tell your guy Arthur and his friends, if these Mostafas and Yehudis come sniffing around any more, I know some Cuban Serbs myself. And they don't use channels. They mostly use cement."

The lamb chops, it turned out, were really very good. You could say special.


When he got back to the room the telephone's message light was blinking again, and this time it was Woody's recorded voice he heard: "Nine in the morning, at the curb outside your place."

Okay. We're moving.

# 24

"LET'S HAVE LUNCH first," Woody said, he being the one driving his cousin's car, a gray Volvo station wagon with the rear third converted to a cage, which Meehan had initially assumed was for inmates, until he got his first, but not last, whiff of dog.

"Sure," Meehan said. By now, he'd grown used to the smell of dog, barely noticed it at all, had not the slightest trouble thinking about food. So they drove on by the turnoff to Spring Road, continuing on up US Route 7 to Sheffield, where they found lunch.

Saturday, October 16, clear pale sky, crisp dry air; they weren't the only people in New York City to decide to drive to New England today, which is why it had taken them three hours to get here. Lunchtime.

Coming back down, Spring Road was on their right, two-lane blacktop heading westward into thick forest, evergreens and maples and a lot of shrubbery, angling upward along the flank of Mount Washington, named for another president, set like a huge shaggy green dunce cap to mark the conjunction of three states. They drove slowly along, the road shrouded by trees, hard to see anything to either side, and after a couple miles there was a car ahead of them, going the same way.

"Traffic," Meehan said.

Looking in the mirror, Woody said, "Somebody behind us, too."

"You wouldn't expect a lot of traffic here," Meehan commented. "Not good news."

Up ahead, the car preceding them signaled for a left. When it then went ahead and made the left, it revealed a guy standing in the middle of Spring Road, wearing a blue blazer, red pants, and a white straw hat. This guy waved for Woody to also turn left.

"The guy behind me," Woody said, "is signaling a left."

"I think we go with the flow," Meehan said.

So they turned left, following the first car, followed by the third. There'd been a sign on a wooden post beside the road where they turned, reading BURNSTONE TRAIL, but it wasn't like a Highway Department sign, the letters being burnt into a rectangle of wood.

Burnstone Trail was thickly flanked by trees, not in a formal planting but obviously groomed and cared for. They also sported red-white-and-blue bunting looped along both sides from tree to tree. Between the trees, stuck into the ground on thin metal feet, were posters in combinations of red and white and blue for several people whose first name seemed to be Reelect.

The car up ahead signaled for another left. "Something," Woody said.

There was a clear space between trees along here, unfestooned by bunting and signs, and behind that space was an open grassy field, tilted a bit uphill toward Mount Washington. About thirty cars were parked in that field, in neat rows, with two guys in white straw hats, blue blazers and red pants ushering each arrival into place. And yes, when the car in front made the turn, there was another similar guy standing in the road, waving them to follow.

They did what all the waving guys suggested, with Meehan noticing that the people getting out of the other cars were all dressed pretty good, but not great, so he and Woody would fit in. He himself was wearing his shirt from last night, and the other new pants, and the new shoes, and his regular zippered cotton jacket that he'd worn into and out of the MCC. Woody was dressed at the same socioeconomic level, so they'd both be all right.

"I don't think there's any point locking," Woody said, as they got out.

When people left their cars, they walked up the gradual slope to the end of the field, where there were more red-white-and-blue people, some of these girls, driving electric golf carts, with one seat beside the driver and two more behind, facing backward.

"You know what this is," Woody said. "This is a political rally. Three weeks before the election, Saturday, no rain, it's a political rally."

"Gets us onto the property," Meehan said.

They rode backward in the cart, along a dirt trail in the woods, which was exactly like life, in that you never knew what was coming, and when they got off at the other end they turned around and there was the house.

Hell of a house. Big and sprawling, it was three stories high, plus attics, all white clapboard, dark green awnings and trim, big porch across the front, big curving porch on the left side. A blacktop road that was no doubt the continuation of Burnstone Trail curled in from the right past the front of the house and continued on into woods on the left, where other structures could just barely be made out.

"Our stuff is gonna be over there," Meehan muttered, as they walked toward the house.

"We shouldn't have had lunch," Woody said.

He was right. Ahead of them, before the road, under tents without sides, were long counters where you could get for free hot dogs, hamburgers, chicken legs, cole slaw, ice cream, soft drinks, wine, and beer. Every one of these counters carried a sign saying what business had donated them, so a whole lot of people were going to have little tax discounts in their future after this day.

It was an outdoor party, that was clear enough, even to the portable toilets discreetly to one side in among the trees. So the area in front of the house was already pretty full of families and couples, everybody trying to deal with a paper plate full of food, a paper napkin, and something to drink, all at once. Some of them were doing this while holding the hand of a child who wanted to go in a different direction.

"Maybe I'll have a hot dog," Woody said, so they both did.

With just a hot dog and a can of beer, and with the paper napkin in your shirt pocket, it wasn't that hard to operate. Meehan and Woody ambled through the people, trending generally leftward, toward where those other structures had been glimpsed off in the woods, and Meehan said, "I don't think with this crowd we could—"

*"Is this on?"*

"Yes!" came a ragged cry from several people.

Woody tapped Meehan's arm and made a head gesture meaning, Let's get farther away from that. So they did.

*"Folks. I'm glad to see this turnout today, and I know Mr. Burnstone is just as glad as I am, and really sorry he couldn't get here for this occasion. . . ."*

They were far enough away now that they didn't actually have to listen if they didn't want to, though some words did creep into their brains unbidden. Meehan said, "All's I know is the stuff isn't in the main house. Looked like there were two, three buildings over this way."

*"—to restore the confidence of the people—"*

They were on the road now, most of the milling partygoers on the grass to their left, the house looming to their right, the speaker some distance behind them up on the front porch, with a lectern in front of him covered with an American flag, the gooseneck microphone on top of that.

"Be nice if we could look in a couple windows," Woody said.

*"—too long in the grip of people playing fast and loose—"*

A bunch of red-white-blue guys on the side porch were unlimbering musical instruments. That they included banjo and clarinet suggested some Dixieland was headed their way. Some saints would soon be marching in.

Beyond the house, Burnstone Trail curved gently rightward among maple and pine trees. At least two buildings were visible back there, one a pocket version of the big house, also in white clapboard, probably a guest house, the other barn-red, therefore a barn. And there might be other structures as well, farther back.

And here, stretched across the trail between big maples, was a golden rope, from which dangled a small metal sign: PRIVATE. And over to the right, seated on a folding chair, big arms folded across big chest, was a guy whose red-white-blue costume did not at all disguise the fact he was a rent-a-cop. He was also looking at Meehan and Woody.

"Let's mosey on back," Meehan said, and so they did.

*"—the protection of the American family against the purveyors of smut and—"*

Yup; When the Saints Go Marching In. Leaning closer to Woody, Meehan said, "I wanna see more of this road."

"And less of that band," Woody said.

They made a wide arc away from the house and back toward the food, picking up another hot dog and beer before angling toward the trail again.

*"—our sons and daughters in uniform—"*

More mixed pine and maple forest, out of which the Trail came a-winding, and across which was another golden rope bearing another go-to-hell sign. "Crowd control," Meehan said.

"Maybe we've seen enough," Woody suggested.

"I know I ate enough," Meehan said, and they headed back toward the house.

*"—the sacred Stars and Stripes!"*

At the beginning, the speaker had been up against people who were already involved in other things, their own conversations, their food, their families, but by sheer doggedness he'd gotten more and more of the crowd to shut up and pay attention—a splinter group was around the corner, paying attention to the band—and even to applaud now and again. Also, more people kept on arriving, so that when Meehan and Woody made their way through they were slowed by quite a crowd between themselves and the route out of here. They quartered slowly through the mob, stitching against the grain.

*"We must build more and better prisons!"*

That got a *big* hand, and even a shout from somebody: "What's a better prison?"

With horror, Meehan realized the shout had come from Woody.

*"One that keeps them longer!"*

Which got both applause and laughter, and another response. As Meehan looked on, aghast, Woody called out, "Don't you believe in rehabilitation?" He was no longer moving toward the dirt path out of here, but toward the speaker on the porch.

Error. Meehan faded back into the crowd, never quite stopping but not giving in to panic either. Woody was in the process over there of breaking about a dozen of the ten thousand rules. Maybe more.

*"We're talking about hardened criminals here."*

"But isn't it prison that hardened them?"

There was the path, just a little farther ahead, just beyond the outermost cluster of listeners. Three or four of the golf carts waited there, with their drivers, but Meehan thought it would be more discreet to walk away at this moment, particularly since everybody, including the golf cart drivers, was enthralled by the debate between Woody and the guy with the microphone.

*"If they weren't criminals, they wouldn't be in prison in the first place."*

"You mean they were criminals when they were born?"

Amazing how Woody's voice carried, even past the golf carts, which Meehan passed now, galloping on the inside but strolling on the outside. Since he well knew that Woody's most usual fashion accessory was the outstanding warrant—don't leave home without one—there was no way that scene could end other than badly.

*"They became criminals when they committed a crime!"*

"Isn't that when they could be wised up, taught how to live right?"

The dirt path angled gently downslope through the trees, the nearest parked cars already visible. Woody hadn't locked the station wagon, but he had the keys with him. It would not be a good idea to go ask for the keys.

*"Don't waste sympathy on those animals! We've got to be tough on them!"*

"Tough? You think you're tough? The joints I've been in, you wouldn't last five minutes! You talk tough out here with all these soft civilians, but— What? What do you people want?"

Meehan was in among the parked cars now, and by golly some of them still had the keys in the ignition. The staff people were all down at the far end, waiting for late arrivals. Meehan wasn't being closely observed, but he was certainly being seen, so he couldn't backtrack or stop to study different cars or do anything but just keep walking, throwing quick glances through car windows along the way.

Here. A nice black Infiniti, a black leather key-holder dangling from the ignition. Without breaking his pace, Meehan opened the driver's door, slid behind the wheel, started the engine.

What a lovely purr this engine made. And when Meehan put it in gear and moved slowly forward, how like a really good powerboat it was, rolling gracefully over the uneven field.

Meehan grinned and waved to the red-white-blues, and they grinned and waved back. At moderate speed, he headed back down Spring Road.

And it didn't smell of dog, either.

# 25

MEEHAN GOT BACK to room 318 a little after nine the next morning to find, yet again, the message light blinking on the telephone. This time, he let it go on blinking while he showered and shaved and brushed teeth. Then, wrapped in a towel, he listened to the message, which was Goldfarb: "Call me."

Well, that was succinct. Meehan hadn't had to memorize Goldfarb's number, since it was okay within the ten thousand rules for him to know it, but it did mean he had to remember where he'd put the piece of paper with the number and address.

In the bedside table drawer, is where, next to the Gideon Bible. He dialed it.

She picked up on the first ring, sounding paranoid: "Who's this?"

"Meehan. You said call."

"Where were you?"

Tricky question. "What do you mean?"

"I left that message four o'clock yesterday."

"I was working," he said. "You know what I mean."

Which was at least partly true. Up to the point he'd driven

away from Burnstone Trail in that clean black Infiniti, he'd been working. After that, the thirty-five miles to the nearest New York City commuter line at Dover Plains, New York, where he'd abandoned the Infiniti without a fingerprint on it, he'd been fleeing. But when he started to chat with the angry woman on the platform, the only other person beside himself headed toward the city on a Saturday afternoon (because she'd broken up with her controlling boyfriend yet again, whose house the country house was, as it turned out), he was on his own time, about which Goldfarb need not concern herself, although in fact the angry woman's—Rosalie, less angry later—apartment was in Goldfarb's general neighborhood.

These irrelevancies, the ten thousand rules suggested, could be left out of the official record; thus: "I was working. You know what I mean."

"Oh," she said, suddenly hushed. "Is it done?"

"No no," he assured her, "that was just to have a looksee. What's up?"

"I need you to come here," she said. "Can you come up here now?"

Lawyer-work on a Sunday? What the hell; stay on her good side. "Sure," he said.

"Okay, listen," she said.

He listened, but she didn't say anything else, so finally he said, "Yeah?"

"Just come up," she said, and broke the connection.

She looked worried. She wore black jeans and a black cashmere sweater and the same monster black-rimmed glasses. She held the door open to say, "Wait, let me get my key," then shut the door in his face and he cooled his heels in the hall a minute till she came back, clutching her keys. She stepped into the hall, pulling the door shut, and he moved toward the elevator, saying, "Where we going?"

"Nowhere. Just stand there."

He looked at her. "In the hall?"

Looking at the key ring in her hand, she said, "The button to unlock the door doesn't work. It's stuck."

"I know."

She leaned toward him, eyes wide behind the big specs: "Did you listen? On the phone?"

He didn't get it. "What do you mean?"

"When I told you listen, did you listen?"

"Yeah, and you didn't say anything."

"The *crackles*," she said.

"The crackles," he repeated. Was there maybe a screw loose in there somewhere?

She leaned even closer, and hissed the next sentence: "They're tapping my phone!"

"Oh, for Christ's sake." Yehudi and Mostafa, had to be.

"I think they probably bugged the apartment, too."

"Let's find a phone booth," Meehan said, "and make Jeffords' morning."

"I knew it was you," Jeffords said, not sounding happy. "On a Sunday morning."

"They're bugging Goldfarb's phone," Meehan said.

"What?"

"And probably the apartment."

"Oh, Jesus, *why* don't they get wise to themselves?"

"Idle hands," Meehan explained, "are the devil's work-shop." Which was in the addendum to the ten thousand rules.

"Well, that explains it, anyway," Jeffords said.

Meehan hated non sequiturs. He said, "I'm glad it does."

"You wouldn't know about this," Jeffords told him, "but a known criminal was nabbed up at, uh, the place you're going."

"Yeah?"

"A known criminal," Jeffords repeated. "At a political rally there. Alfonso Gorman, he's got a record as long as your arm, there were arrest warrants out for him all over."

Alfonso; so that was Woody's civilian name. Meehan said, "They nabbed him at a political rally?"

"That's right."

"Then how come he was the only one they nabbed?"

There was a brief silence until Jeffords got it; then he said, "Very funny. But you see what this means. One of you two must have mentioned it. The name of the place."

Meehan looked at Goldfarb, standing next to him here on Broadway at the phone-on-a-stick, looking as though the half of the conversation she was in on wasn't really nourishing somehow. He said to Jeffords, "Goldfarb doesn't know that name, and I haven't said it."

"Well, *somehow*," Jeffords insisted, "somebody knows *something*, and they sent *somebody*, just the way"—his voice lowered—"just the way we're sending you."

"I'll worry about that," Meehan said, finding no need to bring Jeffords up to date on his own relationship with Woody "Alfonso" Gorman. "You worry about getting those bugs out of Goldfarb's apartment."

"Damn right," Goldfarb said.

"I don't know what I can do on a weekend," Jeffords complained.

"Oh," Meehan said. "Law enforcement's on a five-day week? I wish I'd known that years ago."

"I'll see what I can do," Jeffords promised. "Call me in an hour."

"Goldfarb will."

"Not from the apartment!"

"No, not from the apartment."

"Of course not," Goldfarb said.

Jeffords said, "In the meantime, she should just hang tight, not say anything important to anybody."

"I'll tell her," Meehan said, and hung up, and told Goldfarb, "Call him in an hour. From here, I guess. In the meantime, don't say anything important to anybody."

"Well, it's Sunday," she said.

"Sure."

"I know what," she said. "My mother always says I don't call her enough. I'll call her."

"Let Yehudi and Mostafa listen to an hour of your mother."

"You got it," Goldfarb said.

"Revenge is sweet," Meehan agreed.

# 26

BACK IN ROOM 318, Meehan looked at his shrunken list of initials. Seven left. He hoped the next guy he found had more staying power than Woody.

He felt he needed one more preliminary look at Burnstone Trail, when it wasn't the setting for a Breughel villagers-partying genre picture. He didn't want to go back today, because today would be when the staff was doing cleanup—the part they leave out of the genre pictures—but maybe tomorrow the party staff would be gone and the owner wouldn't yet be back from wherever he'd fled to avoid the hoi polloi, so maybe the job could be done just like that, lickety-split. But first another reconnoiter. With at least one partner, preferably one without an argumentative nature.

Meehan sat on the bed with the phone and the remaining sets of initials, and started his calls.

"Hello?" Tough-guy voice, wary.

"Hi, is Eddie there?"

"This is Eddie. Who's this?"

It was not Eddie; Meehan quietly hung up.

"Bismark residence." Female voice this time, brisk, in a hurry.

"Hi, is Lou there?"

"I don't expect to see Lou for five to fifteen years."

"Oh. Then I'll try again later."

"Hello?" Female voice, motherly.

"Hi, is Bernie there?"

"Oh, you just missed him, I think he's already— Hold on!"

"Sure," he said, hearing shoes run away over a linoleum floor, hearing the woman's receding voice yell, "Bernie! Bernie!" Then silence. Then heavy breathing, out of breath: "No, he's already gone. In the car. He went bowling."

"Bowling."

"He's in a Sunday afternoon league. You know, he has to keep his evenings free."

"Sure."

"He'll be back at six, but that's when we eat supper."

"You don't want me to call at six."

"I could have him call you."

"Nah, that's okay." Very casual: "Where's he bowl?"

"Who's this?" Suddenly not the motherly voice any more.

"It's okay," he assured her. "I'm an old evening pal of Bernie's, my name's Meehan, he may have mentioned me."

"Bernie doesn't mention people," she said, still sounding suspicious, "unless he bowls with them."

"Well, he never bowled with me," Meehan said. "Just tell me, when can I call?"

"Sometimes he— Oh, wait a minute!"

"What?"

But she was off again, cloppety-clop, "Bernie! Bernie!"

Meehan listened to indistinct talk, some of it definitely a male voice, and then what was recognizably Bernie suddenly said in his ear, "Meehan?"

"Yeah. Bernie, hi, how are you?"

"I forgot the ball," Bernie said confidentially. "Can you be-lieve it?"

"Happens," Meehan said.

"I'd forget my head, it wasn't screwed on."

"It isn't!" sallied the woman from away.

Ignoring that, Bernie said, "So what's up?"

"A little something. We could talk, if you're free."

"As a bird," Bernie said. "Where do you wanna talk?"

"You say."

"Come to the bowling alley."

"Yeah?"

"Sure. There's a bar there, always plenty of time between games. Also"—a his voice dropping—"it's so loud in there, you can have a private conversation, you know what I'm saying?"

"I hear you," Meehan said.

The bowling alley, like Bernie's home, was in Queens, which meant Meehan first took a subway under the East River and way to hell and gone out to neighborhoods that haven't seen a stranger since Prohibition ended. From there, he had to take a bus through more neighborhoods of the same, until he debussed at an intersection where Atomic Lanes hunched like a war-surplus airplane hangar opposite him across six lanes of boulevard.

Sometimes a commercial operation's name places it in his-tory. Atomic Lanes would be circa 1946 to 1949, the war over, atomic bombs good, the guys home from the military and wanting to bowl. Most of the Atomic Diners and Atomic Car Washes and Atomic Shoe Repairs from that period were long gone, but here remained Atomic Lanes, unchanged, much like the neighborhood in which it was situated, also still circa 1946 to 1949.

Meehan had an opportunity to do several grafs of his monograph on commercial names in history in his head, just reaching the point of trying to figure out what the first set of changes would have been—Swingers Dry Cleaners?—before the traffic lights changed, and it became possible to cross the boulevard and enter Atomic Lanes.

Noise. That was the first thing that struck him, almost literally, when he pushed through one of the glass doors into the place, a continuous echoing racket bouncing off nothing but hard surfaces, a cacophony he associated with indoor municipal swimming pools.

There were wide steps dead ahead, and a high ceiling full of bright lights beyond. Meehan went up the steps, and the interior revealed itself to him a little more with each step. There must have been 40 lanes 40, every one of them in use. Mostly it was bowling leagues, the teams all in the same shirt, some male leagues, some female, some mixed. Everybody bowled, and everybody talked, and everybody shouted encouragement to everybody else. Everybody shrieked with triumph and cried out in despair.

I couldn't find a hundred Bernies in here, Meehan told himself, but then all at once he did. One, anyway. Six, seven lanes off to the right, dressed like his teammates—all male—in white short-sleeved shirt with maroon stripes on the sleeves and neck and ADDISON'S FUNERAL HOME in maroon italic on the back. That was Bernie there, skinny, quick-moving, mostly bald with pepper-and-salt steel wool around the edges. He was standing on the banquette seat, the better to see what his teammate was going to do with that 7-10 split, which was miss them both, causing four roars of triumph and four wails of agony. Then Bernie grabbed his ball off the return—a sparkly red-white ball, a popular auto color circa Atomic Lanes—and poised himself, waiting for the automatic pin-setter to finish fussing about, which was probably the only real change in here since opening day, the replacement of the pin boys who used to be back there, scrambling desperately out of the way of the oncoming balls.

Meehan walked along the raised aisle behind the banquettes until he was directly behind Bernie and his team, and watched Bernie knock over seven pins, leaving three on the left, then knock down the three. When he turned back to his team, shaking his head, he glanced up and saw Meehan. With a grin, he waved and pointed to something behind Meehan to his right. Meehan looked and it was the bar, open on this side, with tables next to it.

Meehan looked back to nod at Bernie, but Bernie was already again deeply involved with his team, so Meehan went to the bar, got a Rolling Rock, and sat with it at a table where he could watch Bernie's game without entirely understanding it.

By the time Bernie came trotting up, also wearing nonskid bowling shoes the same color as his bowling ball, Meehan was used to the racket. "Whadayasay," Bernie greeted him on arrival, and Meehan heard him fine.

"I say that's a very healthful thing you got going there," Meehan said.

"Yeah, thank God for the bar," Bernie said. "Be right back." And he was, with his own Rolling Rock, saying, "How you been?"

"Bad, until a few days ago," Meehan told him, "but I'll get to that." After having tried out his story on Woody, he'd decided this time to go at it from a different direction. "I got a lead on something," he said, "that Leroy from Cargo's gonna take in a second. And it isn't even that hard to get at."

"Sounds great," Bernie said. "What is it?"

"Antique guns."

Bernie cocked his head. "And again?"

"There's this rich guy up in Massachusetts," Meehan explained, "he collects antique guns from early American wars. Famous collection, goes on tour and everything. Lot of valu-

"Wait'll you hear," Meehan assured him. "The thing is, though, there's a deadline involved. The guy's got his own problems, and we gotta pull the job no later than Thursday."

"*This* Thursday?"

"Yeah."

"Jeez," Bernie said.

"I been up there once," Meehan told him, "and it looks good. I figure we drive up there tomorrow, be certain sure. Could we use your car?"

"Fine," Bernie said. "Only, who's this guy with the deadline?"

So Meehan told him.

When Meehan was finished, there was as much silence at their table as had ever happened in that bowling alley. Then Bernie said, "Took you out of the MCC."

"They needed somebody in a federal facility."

"Is this guy setting you up? Is he who he says he is?"

"He is," Meehan said. "They're paying for my lawyer, six thou already, plus one for me, walking around money. I'm flying in corporate jets contributed to the campaign. They put me up in a United States Parks Department complex down in North Carolina. They're weird, but they're real."

"The weather's supposed to be nice tomorrow," Bernie said. "I'm not tied up, a drive might be nice. Massachusetts, you say?"

"Two and a half hours, no more."

"Okay," Bernie said, and grinned. "What the hell. It's worth it just to be part of that story."

"That's my man."

"So where and when do you want to meet?"

Meehan glanced over toward Mona. "I'll call you in the morning," he said. "We'll set a rendezvous."

able rifles and shit, full of history, Minute Men, Johnny Reb, a
that."

"And you've got a way to get it."

"I know where it is," Meehan said. "I gotta case it a litt
more."

"There's gonna be locks for me," Bernie suggested. He w
a lockman, usually.

"Oh, yeah," Meehan said.

"Sounds interesting," Bernie admitted. "Do you know h
much is in it?"

"I didn't ask Leroy," Meehan said. "You want, give hin
call, tell him you're coming in with me, it's the Burnstone (
lection."

"No, I don't need to," Bernie decided. "Leroy wouldn't
excited if it wasn't pretty good."

"That's what I figured."

Glancing away, Bernie said, "Can you stick around? I'l
back next game."

"Sure," Meehan said.


When next he saw Bernie heading toward the bar, Mee
said to Mona, "There's my friend. I gotta talk to him. So w
on for dinner?"

"Sure," she said, with a grin he was learning to like.
was with an all-girl league.

Meehan paused at the bar for a new Rolling Rock, jc
Bernie, and Bernie said, "You're still a bachelor, huh?"

"No," Meehan told him, "I'm still an ex-husband. Our r
are greater."

"I can see that," Bernie said. "So how did you come 
this gun thing?"

"Well, that's the weird story," Meehan said. "It was br
to me by a guy."

"You can count on him?"

# 27

MEEHAN WAS FINISHING his breakfast at the diner two blocks along the boulevard from Atomic Lanes—the California Dreamin Diner, a more recent vintage—when he saw Bernie pull into the parking lot in a gray Honda Accord with Maryland license plates. Meehan rose, left a dollar on the table, paid the cashier, and went out to where Bernie sat at the wheel, reading the *Daily News*. Meehan slid in beside him and said, "Maryland?"

"Oh, sure," Bernie said. Tossing the paper onto the back seat, steering out to the boulevard, he said, "I put those on if I'm working, going out of town. Those or the Florida plates. I got ID to go with both of them." Stopping at a red light, he grinned and said, "One time, I found out at the end of the day, I had the Florida plates on the car, the Maryland ID in my wallet. Good thing I wasn't stopped."

"Yeah," Meehan said. "You got it right today, though, huh?"

"Ever since then, I double-check."

Bernie drove over to the Van Wyck Expressway, and they did the Whitestone Bridge and the Hutch and on north, and two and a half hours later, as Meehan had promised, they turned off US 7 onto Spring Road. A couple miles later, they came to Burnstone Trail on their left, with a sawhorse across it bearing a sign NO ACCESS. "Aha," Meehan said.

Bernie had stopped, to consider the road and the sign. There was no other traffic on Spring Road today. He said, "That wasn't there, the last time you came up?"

"There was a picnic kind of thing going on last time. Let's see what happens, we go on down Spring Road."

They went on down Spring Road and nothing happened; no houses, no turnoffs, nothing but increasingly thick forest and increasingly steep hill. When the blacktop switched to dirt, Bernie said, "What more do you want to see?"

"Let's go back."

Bernie K-turned, and they looked at the same scenery from the other direction. Driving along, Bernie said, "You think it's better, go in at night?"

"Security's gonna be more serious at night," Meehan said. "And anyway, I wanna give it the double-o."

"Sure."

They kept driving, and then Bernie said, "There it is, up ahead."

"Stop by it," Meehan said, so Bernie did, and Meehan frowned out the Honda window at the sawhorse and the blacktop road beyond it, meandering away. "We gotta get in there," he said.

"Sure," Bernie said.

Meehan frowned some more at the sawhorse, and all at once he said, "Wait a minute. What are we worried about? That isn't a burglar alarm, it's just a sawhorse."

"That's true," Bernie said.

"It doesn't even block the whole road."

"True."

"There's nobody here, nobody going in, nobody coming out."

"Also true."

Meehan looked away from the sawhorse. "You got a map of Connecticut?"

"We're in Massachusetts."

"I know. That's why I want Connecticut."

Bernie considered that for a second, then grinned. "I get it. We're lost."

"That's exactly it."

Bernie rooted around in the pocket of his door, and at last came up with a Connecticut map. "Got it."

"Great. And I tell you what," Meehan said. "Take the key, but don't lock."

" 'Cause we're innocent."

"Just passing through."

They got out of the Honda, walked around the sawhorse, and headed down Burnstone Trail, Bernie folding the map to show northwestern Connecticut, near where they were. All the bunting and election posters had been removed.

After a few minutes, they passed the break in the trees on the left, leading to the field, and Meehan said, "For the picnic, everybody parked in there, and golf carts took them over to the house."

"Pretty snazzy," Bernie said.

"It was a political picnic," Meehan explained, "bring out the faithful. Everything was donated. The rich guy donated his house, or at least the out-front of it, but he was sorry, he couldn't be here."

"Uh-huh," Bernie said.

"I'm hoping he isn't back yet," Meehan said. "What I'd like is nobody here, and no high-tech alarms."

"That would be good."

"If it comes to pass like that," Meehan said, "we'll drive back to the city, get a couple more guys and a truck, come back up tonight, it's all over."

"That wouldn't be bad," Bernie agreed.

They kept walking, and Meehan said, "This is the part of the road I didn't see last time, because of parking back there."

"It's no different from the rest."

"No. There's the house."

It was ahead of them, a lot of massive white through the green trees. They kept walking, and no gold rope was stretched across the road. "This was as far as they wanted you to go, last time," Meehan said. "I mean, the people had to stay in this part, in front of the house." He noticed the food tents were also gone. A neat job had been done, cleaning up.

They walked on by the house, studying it, and Meehan said, "What do you think? Anybody here?"

"No car out front," Bernie said. "No sign of life inside."

"So let's keep going. What we want's gonna be in one of the other buildings."

They went past the house, and the Dixieland band was gone from the side porch, though somehow marching saints did still seem to hover in the air. Meehan smiled broadly when they went past the spot where the golden rope had said, PRIVATE. Off to the right, not only was the security guy gone, so was his chair.

Moving toward the outbuildings, Meehan could now see there were three. The first, white clapboard with the same dark green trim as the main house, looked more and more like a guest house, and the second, barn-red, still looked like nothing but a barn. Beyond the guest house, also white, was a third structure, smaller than the other two, mostly hidden by the others. One story high, it had a bungalow look, with a roof that angled down low over a central front door flanked by windows. There wasn't a porch, just one step up to a platform in front of the door, sided by white railings.

"Something tells me," Meehan said, "our firepower's gonna be in that one back there."

"The road goes right to it," Bernie said.

Which it did; and stopped. Burnstone Trail's end, at the little white bungalow.

They walked to the bungalow, and Meehan went to the window at the right to look in, see what was what inside, and what he saw was a pale face looking out at him. No, it wasn't a reflection of his own face, not unless he'd aged forty years since he'd last checked. He recoiled, and the old guy, a ghostly white figure if you believed in ghosts, waved, then moved away from the window to open the door and lean out and tell them, "Say, you fellows. Come on in."

"We're—" Bernie started, but Meehan overrode him, saying, "Thanks. We were beginning to think the place was empty."

"Couldn't wait to get back, in fact," the old guy said, turning away, walking into the bungalow, trusting them to follow. "Once the riffraff was gone, that is." He had a cultured accent, not quite English, with a gravelly voice.

"A lot of them showed up," Meehan said. He and Bernie entered the bungalow, Bernie stuffing the Connecticut map into his pocket, since somehow the scenario seemed to have changed. Meehan trusted he'd find out what page they were on before too much longer.

The old guy was very tall and lean, and dressed almost completely in white. A white suit, the jacket open over a white shirt open at the collar. Tan Docksiders made for a change of pace. The skin of his face and hands was almost as white as the suit.

By contrast, the bungalow was all dark tones. Indian blankets were thrown over old sofas with wooden arms like paddles. The walls were wood-paneled, with framed Maxfield Parrish prints; nymphs and columns, in some alternate-universe Greece.

"Might as well shut that door," the old guy said, and as Bernie did so, he said, "You boys care for a drink?"

"Sounds good," Meehan said. Until he figured out what the situation was here, it would probably be a good thing to create a friendly aura.

"I've got rye, and I've got bourbon," the old guy told them. "Only American whiskies. And Saratoga water, if you want to ruin it. Now *there* was a battle!" he threw in, with a sudden big smile, his eyes sparkling. "What's your preference, fellas?"

"I'll take rye with some Saratoga water," Meehan said. "It's a little early in the day." Meaning, before lunch.

"Me, too," Bernie said.

"Probably wise. Probably wise."

The old guy opened a big antique mahogany armoire, which had been converted to a bar, complete with sink and tiny refrigerator. Bottles and glasses were on shelves above. Making their drinks, he said, "About the most interesting battle of the war, you want *my* opinion." He kept stopping in his barman activities to gesture, moving armies with his hands. "Redcoats figured on a three-prong advance, south from Canada, north from New York City, east down the Mohawk valley, planned to split the colonies like a pizza pie, Redcoat forces meet at Albany. The force out of New York City never got there; well, what do you expect from New York City? St. Leger, coming down the Mohawk, got as far as Fort Stanwix, but Benedict Arnold drove him back; that was before Arnold turned yellow. Gentleman Johnny Burgoyne, coming down from the north, captured Fort Ticonderoga, didn't do so well at Bennington, and holed up at Saratoga Springs to lick his wounds. Along came General Horatio Gates, held Burgoyne right there, beat him back, forced him to surrender his whole miserable army. October 17, 1777. First time the Americans showed they could do more than snipe and play the guerrilla. They could win a *battle*. Here you are, boys."

This was one of those moments when Meehan wished he could have found history interesting, so he'd have something to say right now. But it was the present that had always fully engaged his attention, with both past and future pretty well off his radar screen. So all he could say, when the old guy handed him a tall glass with a red-white-blue design on it to make it look like a Revolutionary War drum, was, "Thanks."

Bernie also said, "Thanks," but then he said, "I always read it wasn't that Arnold turned yellow, but that he had enemies in Congress, trumped up those court-martial charges against him."

"He should have stood there like a man," the old guy said. He held up his own glass, shorter and fatter than theirs, with LIVE FREE OR DIE on it in black letters (the motto of New Hampshire), in which he was drinking his rye neat, and proposed, "To the Republic."

"Hear, hear," Bernie said, and he and Meehan lifted their glasses as well.

Then Meehan sipped, found the combination not bad, but still a little early in the day, while Bernie said, "That battle of Saratoga, the Americans didn't have as good arms as the British, did they?"

Oh, thank you, Bernie, Meehan thought, while the old guy jumped on the question, saying, "You couldn't be more right! Let me show, let me, just take a look at *this!*" and turned away to open an interior door, while Bernie gave Meehan a huge grin and a spread-hands gesture: what could be better than this?

"Come on in here, boys," the old guy said, switching on the light in the next room.

And here it was. A squarish room completely lined with glass-fronted cabinets containing guns: Kentucky rifles, flintlock muskets, musketoons, breech-loading rifles, carbines, and on shorter shelves a variety of pistols, revolvers, and derringers. The cabinets were gleaming fine wood, and just under the glass of the door fronting each was a discreet brass plate:

COLLECTION OF CLENDON BURNSTONE IV. Which must be the old guy. Clendon Burnstone IV.

Clendon Burnstone IV launched into a whole song and dance about his collection, which Bernie encouraged with the occasional intelligent (apparently) question, while Meehan cased the joint. He had never had the burglee give him a guided tour before, and he found it making him just a bit giddy. Time to bring himself back to earth by recalling one of the most important of the ten thousand rules: If it sounds too good to be true, it is.

Well, whatever the problem was going to be down the line, at this moment there was nothing for Meehan to do but drink in the site of the crime. The door to this room was metal, skillfully painted to look like panelled wood, and it contained three bolt locks. He really couldn't get a good look at the walls, covered as they were by the cabinets, but he suspected they'd be as tough as the door. The floor was a black rubberized material, soft underfoot but no doubt laid on top of concrete. The ceiling was a kind of translucent cream-colored plastic, with lighting behind it that diffused evenly over the room; it too would be fortified against unwanted entry.

The cabinets themselves stood just off the floor, suggesting they might be on casters; the only good news so far. Since the collection occasionally toured, and since each cabinet bore that identifying brass plate, it made sense for there to be casters down there, so it would be easier to move the heavy cabinets around.

Each cabinet door had its own elaborate-looking lock, but none of those mattered. Get into this room with a hammer, that glass was history.

Finally, Burnstone's lecture on his guns and the battles they'd lent themselves to came to an end, and he ushered them back to the front room, shutting but not locking the door, smiling and nodding at Bernie's expressions of delight, preening a little. "I am proud of all that," he admitted. "For one thing, I'm keeping those guns here in America, where they belong."

"That's right," Bernie said. "Do you ever show the collection?"

"Oh, from time to time," Burnstone said, "given the right venue, somewhere decent, where American values are still understood. Richmond, say, possibly Boston. Not one of those kike towns like New York."

"No, I see that," Bernie said.

"I offered it to you fellas, you know," Burnstone said. "Mix it in with a candidate appearance. An *important* candidate appearance."

"Naturally," Bernie said, while Meehan thought, that's who we're supposed to be. People from the campaign committee. Not the CC, Jeffords and Benjamin and all those, but the campaign committee on the Other Side, whatever letters they've made up to describe themselves. Maybe COP; Committee to Oust the President.

"I don't see anything wrong," Burnstone went on, "with injecting a little patriotism into this campaign. *Show* the flag! Remind those mouth-breathers out there, *their* freedom was bought with the blood of patriots!"

"Exactly," Bernie said.

Burnstone shook his head. "But I know how it is, it's all focus groups now, find out what the people want to hear, then say it to them. God forbid you should let your own true feelings show. It's still hard for me to believe, you run an entire presidential election without anybody actually *saying* anything, afraid no matter what they say it'll cost them votes. Well, maybe they're right. Winning's what it's all about, anyway."

"You're right, there," Bernie said.

But, Meehan thought, if he thinks we're from COP, coming to debrief him after the weekend rally, that means *somebody* from COP is headed this way. Which means it would be a good idea to get out of here before the real campaigners show up, because it would be a bad idea to let Clendon Burnstone IV and the Other Side suspect there might be predators in the neighborhood.

"We've taken enough of your time," Meehan said, putting down his unfinished drink. "We really appreciate you showing us your collection, but we ought to get out of here, leave you in peace."

"Well, I was happy to do what I could," Burnstone told them, as he escorted them to the door. "We are coming down to the wire here."

"Yes, we are," Meehan agreed.

"Just a few short weeks, the election will be upon us," Burnstone said, "and by God, I *need* our side to win!"

"Absolutely," Bernie said.

Burnstone opened the bungalow door, accompanied them outside. "Not so much the presidency," he said, "that's just a figurehead, but I need a few fellas in Congress ready to get *my* bill passed."

"That's what we're working on," Bernie assured him.

Speaking confidentially, Burnstone said, "That's the only reason I'm lending myself to all this, you know. For the quid pro quo." He shook his head, heavy with his burdens. "Mingling with the lower orders," he said. "What I normally do with the great unwashed is mostly leave them to themselves. Unwashed they most certainly are, but what makes them great I will never understand." With a wave of a bony hand and an amiable smile, he said, "Nice to have this chat."

# 28

As THEY STEPPED away from the bungalow, Meehan looked over toward the guest house, and said, out of the corner of his mouth, "Pipe that."

What they hadn't been able to see while walking toward the bungalow were the three cars parked in a blacktop area behind the guest house. One was a black Daimler, one an orange Honda Civic, one a green Chevy Celebrity.

"Him, and staff," Bernie suggested.

They walked on, rounding the guest house, aware now that there must be people in there. Meehan said, "I think he's living in the guest house. Suppose the staff lives in?"

"The man's eighty, he doesn't want to be out here by himself."

"I don't want him out here at all," Meehan said.

They followed Burnstone Trail back to the main house, where Meehan said, "I just want to take a look."

"Me, too."

They went up on the porch and looked in windows at mounds of furniture covered by white sheets. Then they went back to the trail and continued on away from there, Meehan saying, "The big house is too big for him, living alone. So he's in the little house, with a couple staff. So how come he doesn't have a family? How come there's no Clendon Burnstone V?"

"Maybe four was enough," Bernie said.

They walked on, the house receding behind them, and Meehan said, "I don't see how we do it with him in the guest house."

"It's a problem," Bernie agreed.

"It's a problem of noise, mostly," Meehan said. "We can't do the job without backing a truck up to the place, and you can't tiptoe a truck." (Not one of the ten thousand rules, just an observation.)

"You can't hide a truck anywhere around here either," Bernie said, "on all these empty roads. You know, to stake the place out and wait for him to leave."

"If he's even gonna leave," Meehan said. "On the other hand, I don't like confrontation."

"I know what you mean," Bernie agreed. "But it's true, every once in a while, the only way to get from here to there is tie up a householder."

Meehan shook his head. "I'd like to find another way."

"I've seen that collection now," Bernie said, "and I want it. And I want to take it away from *him*."

"I know."

Bernie frowned. "But, you know," he said, "I didn't see the other part. This package of yours."

"Oh, it'll be there," Meehan said. "I noticed, some of those cabinets had little drawers."

"For bullets," Bernie said, "flintlocks, gunpowder pouches, things like that. He said so."

"The package'll be in there, too," Meehan said, and saw a car coming down the road toward them, a maroon Cadillac Seville. "Gotta deflect these guys," Meehan said, and held up a hand.

There were two men in the Cad, stout, florid-faced, in suits and ties. They stopped, and the driver buttoned his window down, and Meehan leaned close to say, "You fellas from the Committee?"

"That's us," said the driver. "Owen Grassmore, and this is Herb Greedly."

"Fred Leeman," Meehan said, pointing at himself, "and this is Dave Harkin."

"How'd you do," everybody said.

Meehan said, "We were just up there to talk about the band. They think they might have left a banjo behind."

"It's amazing," Grassmore said, "how often that happens."

"And if you'll take a piece of advice," Meehan said, "you won't go see the old man, not today."

Grassmore looked confused. "We're supposed to pay a courtesy call, thank the man for the use of the property."

"I understand that," Meehan said, "but right now he's hopping mad."

Bernie added, "Talking about riffraff, mouth-breathers, all over his property."

"Oh, God," Grassmore said, "I've seen him when he's like that."

"The great unwashed," Meehan said. "He'll calm down after a while, but at this point, you remind him of the rally, you'll just make things worse. Like we did."

Greedly, the other one, leaned over to say, "That's one miserable old man, you want my opinion."

"I agree completely," Meehan told him.

"If the son of a bitch didn't have four hundred million dollars," Greedly said, "nobody on this earth would talk to him."

"His own family won't talk to him," Grassmore said.

"*Talk* to him?" Greedly offered a bark of angry laughter. "The whole family's *suing* each other!"

"I do hate the rich," Grassmore said, "but we need their money."

"Well, you can spare yourselves some trouble," Meehan told them, "if you hold off the courtesy call until later in the week."

"When he's calmed down," Bernie said.

"Calmer, anyway," Meehan amended. "Say Friday. He ought to be all right by Friday. Bearable, anyway."

"Thanks for the warning, fellas," Grassmore said. "I shall certainly take your advice."

Greedly said, "That your car out by the road?"

"It's mine," Bernie told him.

Grassmore said, "You want a ride back out to it?"

"That'd be great," Meehan said, and he and Bernie climbed into the comfy back seat.

"Happy to help," Grassmore said, panting as he steered endlessly through a lot of backing and filling to turn the big car around.

Greedly grinned at them from up front. "After all," he said, "we're all in the same party, all in the good cause together. It's not like you're with the Other Side."

"Bite your tongue," Meehan said, and they all laughed.

# 29

BACK IN THE Maryland Honda, headed south, having said grateful goodbyes to Grassmore and Greedly, and made sure no one from COP (or whatever they were) would approach Burnstone IV before Friday—when either the caper would already have been pulled or Meehan would be well on his way to Idaho—they discussed the possibilities, of which there didn't seem to be any.

"We can't go in silent," Bernie said.

"I know that," Meehan agreed. "But you know and I know he's got to have some kind of security there, in the bungalow and in the guest house, too. Phone alarms to the local law, at the very least. I don't want to try busting in, kidnapping everybody, tying everybody up . . ."

"I'm with you," Bernie said. "Always too much chance of violence, things going bad. And an iffy thing to do to an eighty-year-old man, give him a heart attack, then it's murder one."

"Kidnapping, now murder." Meehan shook his head. "All's I want to do is a little burglary."

"Not with Burnstone and his staff on the property," Bernie

said. "So either we go in when he's there, and keep him quiet somehow, or we get him *off* the property somehow."

"You're back to kidnapping," Meehan pointed out.

They came to an intersection, routes 7 and 44. Bernie stopped and said, "Which way do we go?"

"That's the question, isn't it?" Meehan said.

Out of Massachusetts, a dog-ear of Connecticut, down New York's Taconic Parkway. Bernie drove, and Meehan frowned at the autumnal world out there without quite seeing it. He knew the lay of the land now; so how about a way to pull the job?

He found himself thinking about Sherlock Holmes, whose top number one in his own personal ten thousand rules was, Exclude the impossible, and whatever's left, however improbable, is the answer. Okay, exclude the impossible. Can't go in without being heard, can't confront the household without too much risk of unwanted violence and unknown alarm systems. So what's left? A silent helicopter.

Fine. Forget Sherlock Holmes, who in any case is *really* on the Other Side.

Breaking a silence of nearly an hour's duration, Bernie glowered out at the Taconic Parkway, almost empty on a Monday afternoon, and said, "I *really* want those guns."

"Yes," Meehan said. "And I really want to not go back to the MCC. And I probably don't want to go to Idaho, either. Everybody wants something, we all want something. Even Burnstone probably—"

"I guess so," Bernie said. "Even at his age."

"Hush," Meehan said.

"You know, we forgot all about lunch?"

"Hush!"

Bernie gave him a curious look, then faced front and said, "You've got a scheme."

"I've got a thread," Meehan said. "I'm following it. Does it lead me to a scheme? Turn around, we have to go back. We *know* what Burnstone wants."

"We do?"

"He wants to make a speech," Meehan said.

This time, they drove around the sawhorse and on down Burnstone Trail, taking the blacktop jug handle around to the back of the guest house, where they parked among the Daimler, the Honda, and the Chevy. As they got out of their own (different model) Honda, the guest house rear door opened and a worried-looking woman with two yellow pencils stuck into the gray-and-black bun atop her head as though it were Secretary's Day among the geishas leaned out to say, "May I help you?"

"We were here before," Meehan told her. "From the Committee. I'm Owen Grassmore and this is Herb Greedly. Mr. Burnstone still in with the gun collection?"

"Mr. Burnstone," she informed them, with a proprietary chill, "is finishing his midday repast."

"Well, I think he'll want to see us," Meehan informed her back. "Tell him it's Grassmore and Greedly, the fellows he showed the gun collection to this morning, and we have a request to make of him."

"No doubt you do," she said. "You political fellows always do have a request to make, don't you?"

"Yes, ma'am," Meehan agreed.

"One moment."

She went back inside and Bernie said, "I like her as much as I like him."

"We won't be dating much," Meehan said, and the door opened again so Burnstone himself could come out, his LIVE FREE OR DIE glass in his hand and a rather stained white napkin tucked into his shirt at the neck. "Hello, again," Meehan said.

Burnstone came down the two cement steps to the black-top, saying, "You fellows forget something?"

"No, sir," Meehan said. "A situation just came up, and we wondered if you could help us out."

"For the party?" Burnstone stood straighter. "Anything I can do," he said.

"Well, sir," Meehan explained, "there's going to be a big lunchtime rally on Wednesday over in Bellwether, and Senator Windsor was gonna give the main speech there, but we just got word he came down with bronchitis. And I remembered, this morning, you said you'd be willing to speak if the need should arise, and—"

"Speak?" Burnstone's eyes glittered, but then the glitter faded, and he said, "You mean, read some twaddle already done up, equality for housemaids, all that."

"Oh, no, sir," Meehan said. "There's nothing prepared, and no time to prepare anything. Mr. Greedly and I talked it over, and you're such a patriot, with such a grounding in American history, it just seemed natural you could talk about whatever you wanted, and the crowd would eat it right up."

"Particularly," Bernie said, "this particular crowd."

"Oh?" Alert, Burnstone said, "And who are these folks?"

"The F A R," Bernie said.

Burnstone, doubtful, repeated the initials. "I'm not sure I know them."

Bernie said, "They're the Friends of the American Revolution. It's an organization for people whose ancestors *would* have fought in the Revolution—"

"On our side," Meehan interpolated.

"Well, sure," Bernie said. "Would have fought on our side in the Revolution if they'd got here on time. It's for people who, because of the accident of birth—"

"And geography," Meehan interpolated.

"—don't qualify for the DAR or the SAR. So for them there's the FAR."

"Well, that sounds damn decent," Burnstone said. "They sound like good folks."

"Landed, mostly," Bernie said. "Good northern European stock, mostly." He leaned closer. "Our sort," he said, with a wink.

"I get you," Burnstone said, and tapped his finger to the side of his nose. "I look forward to meeting these people."

Meehan said, "Then you'll do it? You'll be a real lifesaver."

"I can see it's my duty," Burnstone assured him. "Tell me where to be, and when, and I'll be there."

"It's probably an hour's drive from here," Meehan told him. "You know, over in Bellwether."

"Don't think I know the place."

"We'll send a limo for you," Meehan promised. "Pick you up about eleven, give you a good lunch while you're there. How many folks you got on the property here?"

"Just the three," Burnstone said. "Miss Lampry you already met, is my personal assistant. Then the Joads do the cleaning and cooking and so on."

"Bring them along," Meehan urged him. "There'll be plenty of room in the limo, and the bigger a showing we can make at the event, the bigger a showing we'll get in the media."

"Bring them?" Burnstone looked uncertain.

Bernie said, "The Joads can ride up front with the chauffeur; plenty of room."

The skies cleared; Burnstone smiled broadly on them both and said, "It sounds like a wonderful outing. I've a number of issues I could talk about."

"I'm sure you have," Meehan said.

"The limo," Bernie said, "will be here Wednesday morning at eleven."

"I'll be raring to go," Burnstone told them, and toasted them with LIVE FREE OR DIE.

Friendly goodbyes were said all around. Then, back in the car, headed away from the houses, Bernie said, "Meehan, enough is enough. I just got to have lunch. It's almost three o'clock. I'm so hungry I was about ready, back there, to eat his napkin."

# 30

OVER LUNCH AT a place in Sheffield, Mass., they discussed what they had and what they needed to get. "First, a limo," Meehan said, "and a chauffeur." Bernie, trying to eat an entire double cheeseburger all at once, nodded.

"Then we also need a truck," Meehan said, and Bernie nodded.

"Now, neither of us can be the chauffeur," Meehan said, "because Burnstone's already seen us," and Bernie nodded.

"So you and me are in the truck, which I guess one of us is driving," Meehan said, and Bernie nodded and pointed at him.

"So I'm driving the truck," Meehan said, "and you're dealing with locks and alarms," and Bernie made a doorknob-twisting gesture.

"I'm wondering," Meehan said, "if we try to wheel the cabinets out or just bust the glass and take the guns," and Bernie swung an imaginary hammer.

"Yeah, okay, we got no use for the cabinets," Meehan said, "since Leroy's gonna break the set up anyway, so the next question is, do we carry all that stuff ourselves or do we bring in more muscle?" and Bernie pointed at Meehan and then at himself.

"Well, I understand your saying that," Meehan agreed, "because that means there's more in it for us if we've just got us two and the chauffeur, but that's a lot of heavy guns there," and Bernie tapped the face of his wristwatch.

Meehan nodded. "Sure, we got time, at least an hour, maybe more. So okay, it'll just be the two of us at the place, with the truck. So now what we need is the chauffeur," and Bernie raised a hand, palm outward, for Meehan to pause.

Meehan paused, and watched Bernie gulp down a big swig of diet soda. Then Bernie said, "I got the chauffeur."

"You do? Why didn't you say?"

"I just did," Bernie said. "Bob Clarence. You know him?"

"I don't think so."

"He's a driver," Bernie said. "Terrific. Nerves of steel. Never drives away from the bank without the people he brought there."

"Good man."

"And the thing about him is," Bernie said, "he's already got a chauffeur suit. See, that's the way he sets up, a lot of the time, to do the job. You see a car in front of the jewelry store, motor running, you say, 'Hey, what's goin' on?' Then you see the guy in the chauffeur suit at the wheel, you say, 'Oh.' Like you know something."

"This guy sounds great," Meehan said.

"He is," Bernie said. "I'll call him when we get back to the city, see if he's available Wednesday."

"Then call me at the motel."

"Will do." Bernie grinned. "And here's the best part, given who we're dealing with here."

"Yeah?"

"Bob's black," Bernie said.

Meehan grinned like a carp. "You are gonna make Clendon Burnstone IV very happy," he said.

"For a little while," Bernie said.

# 31

EVERY TIME MEEHAN entered room 318 the telephone message light blinked at him. This time, when he pushed the button, there was first a spectral voice to tell him he had three messages, and then all three of them were from Goldfarb:

1) "Our hearing is set for eleven o'clock Tuesday morning in chambers at Family Court in Queens. We should go over the situation together ahead of time. Give me a call."

2) "Meehan, we really have to make contact here, before we go to court. Call me, will you?"

3) "Where *are* you? I left one message yesterday, one message this morning, you're *still* not anywhere, where do you *go* all the time? Or did you decide to take off to Idaho after all? There's no point my going out to court tomorrow if you aren't with me, since the whole point is, you're supposed to be in my *custody*. Where *are* you?"

So he called her, and when she said an irritable, "Hello?" he said, "Well, I was about my employer's business, and you don't want to know about that. So I'm here now."

"I had just about given up on you," she said.

"Most people do," Meehan said. He was used to it.

She sighed, but stayed on message: "Can you come with me to court tomorrow morning?"

"Sure. Eleven A.M.? No problem."

"We should get there early, probably leave the city nine-thirty." (The boroughs outside Manhattan are technically parts of New York City, but every New Yorker going out there describes it as "leaving the city," which in fact it is.)

"Fine," Meehan said. "Subway again?"

"You've been on the subway."

"That part was legal," he told her. "In fact, almost everything I did today was legal."

"Are you going to volunteer information?"

"Absolutely not."

"Good. We should discuss ahead of time."

"On the subway?"

"You can't have a discussion on the subway," she told him. "Buy me dinner."

"Me? You're the one with the six thou."

"I've been carrying you, Meehan," she said. "It's your turn."

He shrugged, though she wouldn't be able to see him do it. "Yeah, sure, okay," he said. "But not the place Jeffords took us."

"I realize that. You pick it, some crappy greasy spoon somewhere. I'll bring the Tums."

"I know a great Caribbean place downtown," he said, "got goat elbow."

"Goat— You're putting me on."

"No, I'm not. It's the part of the goat leg that bends, I don't know what you call it, I call it the elbow. With the spices and everything, it's terrific."

"Everything I hear about downtown," she said, "reminds me why I live uptown."

"So slum a little," he said.

"What time you want to meet?"

\*       \*       \*

The restaurant, on a side street in the West Village, with its happy crowd of multilingual uninhibited diners shouting over the reggae that blared from speakers in every corner of the ceiling, was only slightly louder than a subway car taking a curve, but the goat elbow was as Meehan had described it, and the margaritas weren't bad either. For slumming, Goldfarb wore black ankle boots, black wool slacks, and a bulky plum-colored sweater. The monster eyeglasses were the same. Meehan was in his usual zippered jacket and stuff.

"We can't discuss in here!" she yelled, after they'd yelled their order to the tall skinny Jamaican waiter.

"What?" he yelled.

"We can't discuss in here!"

"Later!"

"What?"

He used his fingers to show two people walking, and pointed out to the street. She nodded, and they had dinner, and he paid with cash, because that was what he had. Then they went out to the cool night, the quiet Village streets, and Goldfarb said, "Okay, goat elbow is very good, but we were supposed to have a discussion."

"We can walk a ways," he said.

They walked, and she said, "There's already been a lot done on the case, but that was just paperwork. For this last step, you have to be physically present in front of the judge and that's the tricky part, because she's a juvenile court judge."

Meehan said, "But she's in on the scam, isn't she?"

"Not exactly," Goldfarb said.

The night was cool, but not bad. Trees dimmed much of the illumination from the streetlights, traffic was light, and other people, in couples or groups, also strolled through the calm darkness. The West Village is an oddly peaceful corner of Manhattan, without the normal traffic and crowds and neon, its narrow maze of streets too much of a challenge for tourists and cabbies alike. The Caribbean restaurant they'd just left was probably the loudest spot within a mile.

Given the shadowed streetlights and muffled traffic and strolling people and crisp air, Meehan knew this was a situation to be considered generically romantic, but he also knew it was a moment wasted. In any other circumstance, strolling with an okay woman after dinner, he'd probably put the moves on, but this was none of those circumstances. To begin with, Goldfarb was a lawyer, and between the felon and the attorney there were lines not to be crossed. In the second place, his first relationship with her had been in the MCC, and there was still something of the MCC lawyer-client conference in all of their meetings, which would put a chill on any kind of warm inclination. Also, there were those monster glasses. And, over and above all the rest, she was Goldfarb.

And talking. "This judge," she was saying, "T. Joyce Foote, only knows what the paperwork says as it comes across her desk. And what it's going to say is, on Friday, while we were flying up from Norfolk and my apartment was filling up with spies, for God's sake, Bruce Benjamin's people went to the district attorney upstate in New York, and got her to move to have your case put under her jurisdiction, meaning state instead of federal, using your own argument that there was no external evidence of government involvement with the truck and its contents on the truck itself."

"Like I said."

"Like you said," she agreed. "Now, normally the federal prosecutor would fight such an encroachment, but this time the word had gone out."

"The fix was in," Meehan suggested.

"Whatever," she said. "The point is, he didn't object, and the change went through. That done, the upstate DA graciously consented to pass you on to an outer borough New York City

DA, since you were already physically incarcerated within the city limits."

"I bet," Meehan said, "normally that would have been a turf fight, too."

"You know it. Anyway, this morning I applied for your release into my custody, since you were being improperly held in a federal facility with no federal charges pending against you, and in *that* paperwork you became a minor."

"Huh," he said.

She shrugged, as though to say she wasn't making a big deal out of it but it was a big deal, and said, "That's how I got custody. *Out* of the MCC because you're not a federal prisoner, *into* my custody because you were being improperly held, and all at once the reason it was improper to hold you in the MCC is because you're a minor."

"Three-card monte," Meehan suggested.

"Very similar. Now," she said, "a lot of people at both the federal and state level had to squint real hard when they passed that paperwork along, but everybody had been given to understand there were good reasons known only on high, and that absolutely no backlash would ever occur. So now the last step is Juvenile Court Justice T. Joyce Foote, who will take one look at you and know you're not in the normal way of PINS under her jurisdiction."

"I'm not a PINS," Meehan said, feeling blank.

"Person In Need of Supervision. It's the custodial phrase when dealing with minors."

Meehan nodded. "Okay. So all she knows is the paperwork, she looks at me and says, 'You're no Pin,' and boots paperwork right back out of her court."

"Chambers," Goldfarb said. "I wouldn't parade you in juvenile court, believe me. And no, she won't boot it back, because she will see that everybody else, including people with more sway and import than her or anybody else in juvenile court has dogs, when the phone rang and it was Bernie, sounding very troubled: "He could meet at midnight."

"Good," Meehan said.

"Jeez, Meehan," Bernie said. "To tell you the truth, I don't *wanna* drive into the city at midnight."

"You've become suburban, Bernie," Meehan told him.

"It's the real me, coming to the surface," Bernie said. "Whyn't you meet him without me?"

"How would I recognize him?"

"I'll describe him to you, and you to him."

Meehan wasn't sure about this. The way it worked, since you were in the process of something illegal, the way the ten thousand rules laid it out, you do not meet with a stranger. You meet with somebody you know who *knows* the stranger and can introduce you.

But Bernie had, as Meehan had pointed out, turned suburban in his middle years. There was no getting him into Manhattan at midnight, not even on a Monday. So Meehan sighed and said, "Okay, describe him."

"He's black."

Meehan waited. Then he said, "I knew that part. So where are we meeting, a Klan convention, he's the only black guy there?"

"No, he wants to meet at a garage on a Hundred Twenty-fifth Street and Amsterdam Avenue."

"That's Harlem," Meehan said.

"Yeah, sure," Bernie said. "It's an all-night gas station garage, I guess he hangs out there or something."

"He's not gonna be the only black guy at a Hundred Twenty-fifth Street and Amsterdam Avenue," Meehan said. "Give me more description."

"He's maybe forty, wiry, not too tall, always wears a hat, maybe a cap. I think he's bald under there."

"Well, I'll try it," Meehan said.

already signed off on it. And that's when *I* explain there are other humanitarian reasons for this special treatment, or perhaps you're just a major turncoat about to testify against everybody in the world. We'll shade between superfink and a wasting disease, without getting specific about anything, because we don't *have* to get specific. Are you following me?"

"No," Meehan said.

"All right, fine," she said. "Your job, in front of Judge Foote, is to look hangdog but shifty, which I think you can do, and maybe toss in a little physical weakness as well. Answer questions briefly, volunteer nothing."

"I have volunteered nothing," Meehan told her, "every day of my life."

"Hold the course," she advised. "Tomorrow morning gets rid of your legal troubles."

"Hallelujah," he said.

"However," she told him, "do remember that you are, or will be, on probation, and in my custody. There's still a leash on you. If you try to pull a fast one, run away, fail to deliver to Jeffords and Benjamin, *everything* that was done gets undone, and you're on your way back to the MCC."

"Gotcha."

Light bounced off her spectacles as she studied him. "You are going through with this, aren't you?" she asked. "All the way."

"All the way," he agreed.

"Good." She peered ahead, where much brighter light gleamed at the next intersection. "That looks like Seventh Avenue."

He looked around to orient himself. "Yeah, I think it is."

"We can find a cab there," she said, picking up the pace. "Come on, I'll drop you."

As they walked, Meehan looked back at the leafy darkness from which they were emerging. Too bad, really.

# 32

Every time, every single time. Every time Meehan walked into room 318, there was that red light on the telephone, blinking like a reflex. Well, this time it couldn't be Goldfarb, whom he'd just left in the cab out front, so he went over to see what was what, and the nonvoice informed him he had two messages. Great to be popular.

The first was from Bernie: "We could meet Bob at eleven in the morning, out here. Okay?" Bob would be the driver, Bob Clarence.

And the second message was from Jeffords: "I understand you're getting your day in court tomorrow. Congratulations. I'll be coming up in the afternoon to get a progress report. Call me on my, uh, private line when you get out of court."

Progress report. Tomorrow was filling up, which Meehan could have done without.

The clock radio bolted to the bedside table read 9:43. Bernie would be up, but would he be in or out? Meehan found the number in his memory bank, dialed it, and the missus answered. He said, "It's me, Meehan, again. Is Bernie around?"

"He's watching one of his favorite shows."

PUT A LID ON IT

"Oh. Does he want to call me back?"

"Hold on, I'll ask," she said, and clomp-clomped away, and the next voice he heard was Bernie: "You got my message."

"I don't want to take you away from your favorite show."

"It stinks, actually," Bernie said. "We on for tomorrow?"

"I can't," Meehan told him. "I gotta go to juvenile court." When Bernie responded with nothing but silence, Meehan added, "It's okay, it's part of the process."

Bernie said, "Do I wanna know what process?"

"The process we discussed, that has me here instead of downtown."

"Okay, fine, skip it. Afterward?"

"Well, no, I got another thing then."

"Meehan, we're talking about doing this thing day after tomorrow."

"I know that."

"Bob needs a meet, he needs the story from you."

"But he's free, he can do it."

"Maybe. He'll decide after he hears the story from you."

Meehan frowned at the clock radio. "How about tonight?"

"Tonight? He's in the city, he won't want to come out here tonight."

"Bernie," Meehan said gently, "I'm in the city, too."

There was another little silence from Bernie, but this time Meehan waited him out, and finally Bernie said, "You mean, should drive into the city tonight."

"After your favorite program."

"No, screw that, I hate that show, it's just habit. Let me see can I reach Bob, and I'll call you back."

"Fine," Meehan said, and spent the interval with the television set, trying to figure out which of these dogs on view was Bernie's favorite program.

All the dogs were ending, to be replaced by the ten o'clock

*     *     *

"A Hundred Twenty-fifth and Amsterdam," Meehan said.

The cabby, a recent immigrant from Latvia, turned to look at Meehan through the bullet-proof Plexiglas. "You sure?"

"Positive," Meehan said. "There's a garage there that—"

"Oh," the Latvian said, "you're gonna drive a hack. Sure. I still gotta charge you."

"That's okay," Meehan said, and sat back. If he said he *wasn't* gonna drive a hack, what would that do? Prolong the conversation.

The Latvian's conclusion, it turned out, had not been that improbable a jump. Just off the intersection was an oasis of bright light amid the surrounding semidarkness, and this bright light gleamed all around a gas station and parking building that called itself, according to the big metal sign out by the street, UPTOWN 24/7. Meehan got out of the cab and looked at the taxis parked all around the place, the gas station cashier behind his Plexiglas window in the face of the brick building, the parking entrance next to the cashier, and the sign on the wall saying you could also rent a car here, if you wanted. Everything automotive, under one roof.

Meehan walked over to the parking entrance, and inside was an open concrete-floored space with DRIVE UP and STOP HERE signs, and more taxis parked in the area in the back, and a concrete ramp leading upward, and off to the side a set of little offices behind big windows. Half a dozen black guys in white shirts, black pants and black bow ties stood around in clumps, talking; the staff. One of them wore a New York Yankees cap, frontward. He was about forty, wiry, not too tall.

It was a different one who came toward Meehan, hand out for a claim check, saying, "Evening."

"Hi," Meehan said. "I'm here to see Bob Clarence."

The air very subtly shifted all around him. People kept talking, but they weren't listening to each other any more, they were listening to Meehan. People kept facing one another, but out of the sides of their heads they were looking at Meehan. The guy who'd wanted his claim check dropped that hand to his side, frowned, looked thoughtful, then shook his head. "I don't think I know him," he said. "Bob what?"

"Sure," Meehan said, and went over to stand in front of the guy in the Yankees cap, who kept talking about NASCAR racing with his friends until Meehan said, "Bernie says, under that hat, you're probably bald."

Bob Clarence gave Meehan an outraged look. "He does? Where's he come off with *that* shit?"

Meehan leaned in to peer at Clarence's hair around the edges of the cap. "I thought black guys never got bald," he said.

"You can lay off lookin at my head," Clarence said. "And you can tell me who the hell you're supposed to be."

"Meehan," Meehan said, and shrugged. "If there's a password, Bernie didn't tell me."

"Bernie doesn't know everything," Clarence said, still irritated. "Come on. Later," he told his friends, and led Meehan back outside, where he pointed westward and said, "We'll grab some Chinese."

"I already had Caribbean tonight," Meehan told him, walking beside him, the oasis of light receding behind them. "Goat elbow, very good."

Clarence looked interested. "Down in the West Village?"

"You know the place?"

"The goat is good," Clarence agreed. As they walked he took off and pocketed his clip-on bow tie, unbuttoned his top shirt button, and folded his shirtsleeves back. "You're gonna like this Chinese," he said. "They do stuff with shrimp you won't believe."

There are worse things in this world, Meehan thought, than two dinners in one night. "Lead on," he said.

The shrimp was very good, and so were the spring rolls, and so was the whole baked fish. They had Tsingtao Chinese beer, and Clarence wielded his chopsticks like samurai swords, wearing his hat while he ate, and through the meal Meehan told him his story. When he finished, Clarence said, "They'll never do that for a black guy. Never."

"They don't do it for a lot of white guys," Meehan assured him.

Clarence drank Tsingtao and brooded. "I'm not sure I *wanna* help this president," he said.

"I figure I'm helping *me*," Meehan told him. "The president's piggy-backing."

"But if the law walks in on us," Clarence said, "this president of yours isn't gonna know us."

"That's why we gotta do it right," Meehan told him, "with exactly the right people."

"Tell me about this old guy we're gonna heist," Clarence said. "I don't know if I like that, boostin from some old guy."

"Well, you're gonna love him," Meehan said. "He thinks everybody's scum except him. The great unwashed, he says."

Clarence considered that. "Anti-black, you mean?"

"Clendon Burnstone IV doesn't fine-tune," Meehan said.

"Well, maybe that's okay," Clarence decided, "if that's the way he is."

"He was on our side in the Revolution," Meehan said, "but he's been against us ever since."

"Okay, fine. You got a scheme for how to do this?"

Meehan told him the scheme. Clarence made an Olympic symbol on the shiny hard tabletop with his Tsingtao bottle while he listened, then finished the beer and said, "That's a mean thing to do to a guy that age."

"It's the meanest thing I could think of."

"I tell you what," Clarence said. "I'll drive for you, I'll do this thing, but I'm gonne be in that limo with that old man a pretty long time, and if I decide that's too mean a thing to do, old guy like that, I'll just drive him right back home, right into the middle of your caper, let you people sort it out."

"I'm not worried," Meehan said.

"Okay," Clarence said. "Just so you know how I feel."

"I know how you feel."

"Let's see what fate thinks about all this," Clarence said, and reached for one of the fortune cookies in the middle of the table.

Meehan took the other, cracked it open, and read the slip of paper: "A silver tongue is more valuable than a golden sword." And what was that supposed to mean?

Clarence said, "Listen," and read: "Age must be honored, but youth must be served."

Meehan said, "Okay, whose side are they on?"

"What does yours say?"

So Meehan read it to him. They both thought about this array of Oriental wisdom for a while, and then Clarence said, "Fuck it. We'll just do it and see what happens."

# 33

Okay; just once, when he got back to 318 from meeting with Bob Clarence, the message light wasn't blinking on the bedside phone, but at nine the next morning, when he returned to the room after a breakfast in the neighborhood, there it was again, *red-red-red*, and turned out to be Goldfarb: "I'll pick you up in front of your place at nine-thirty."

So he went down to the street at nine-thirty, and she wasn't there on the sidewalk, but a minute later she was there, in a limo. Waving at him from the back seat of a limo, with a black chauffeur in uniform at the wheel. Feeling a weird moment of paranoia or surrealism or something, Meehan bent to check, but the chauffeur wasn't Bob Clarence. Still, to have a life suddenly full of limos was kind of unsettling.

Meehan slid into the back seat next to Goldfarb, who grinned at him, said, "Good morning," and before he could answer leaned forward to call to the chauffeur, "Okay."

They pulled into traffic, the chauffeur trying to get over to the left lane, and Goldfarb grinned at Meehan again, saying, "Not bad, huh?"

"No, not bad," Meehan agreed. "I thought we were gonna do the subway, so this is not bad."

"Jeffords called me last night," she said.

"Yeah, he left a message in my room. He's gonna be up here, he wants me to call him and give him a report after court."

"I know about that," Goldfarb said, as the chauffeur managed the slow and tricky left onto Forty-second Street. "What he called *me* about was to authorize me to hire this car this morning, to take you out to your court date. That's the word he used, authorized."

"Meaning he'll pay you back."

"Exactly."

"How come?" Meehan asked. "This doesn't seem like the Jeffords I know."

"He finally believes," she said, "that you're actually going to do it, and what he said to me was, he wants to keep you happy."

"Well, that's nice," Meehan said. "We're seeing eye to eye there. I want to keep me happy, too."

"Chambers" was a little room about the size of the box a grand piano might come in, with a low ceiling crisscrossed by cables and pipes, and two tall narrow dirty windows with a view, beyond an air shaft, into a larger brightly fluorescented room lined with rows of gray metal filing cabinets, among which people appeared and disappeared, moving slowly and bearing handfuls of paper and facefuls of distraction, like laboratory animals kept in the maze just a little too long.

Chambers itself was very crowded, with a stubby metal desk facing away from the windows, two tall filing cabinets on the left, two wooden armchairs facing the desk, and a library table on the right piled with children's books and magazines and soft toys. The dark wood entrance door was in the wall opposite the air shaft, flanked by bookshelves floor to ceiling, crammed with law books and more kid lit.

Judge T. Joyce Foote, whose office this was, deep in the bowels of this massive old stone government building far in the outer boroughs, rose to greet them when they entered, and Meehan thought immediately that she looked like Mrs. Muskrat in some of those kiddy books over there, who would live in a tree trunk, with curtains on the windows, and make pies. She was black, very stout, short, dressed fussily in purple and ribbons. On her face were eyeglasses the exact rebuttal of Goldfarb's black-rimmed monsters, being delicate glass ovals suspended in the slightest possible lines of golden wire. She smiled a greeting, but there was something sharp and calculating in the eyes behind the granny specs. She was a Mrs. Muskrat who knew very well how to live deep in these woods.

She smiled at Goldfarb and then at Meehan, and then at something in between them, or behind them, at waist level. As the smile became confused, Meehan realized she was looking for the child. Should he raise his hand?

No. Goldfarb had brought paperwork with her, in a manila folder that she now extended toward the judge, saying, "Here you are, Your Honor, the documents."

Taking them, frowning, the judge said, "Francis Xavier Meehan?"

"Me, Your Honor," Meehan said, and actually did raise his hand partway.

Before the judge could react, Goldfarb said, "Your Honor, I'm Elaine Goldfarb, the attorney in the case."

The judge hefted the manila folder in her hand, while she gave Meehan the skeptical look he deserved. "With the explanation, I presume."

"It's all in the documents, Your Honor," Goldfarb told her, with a little hospitable gesture inviting the judge to open the folder and wade right on in.

"Well, sit down," the judge said, welcoming and dubious at the same time, and sat down herself as they did. "Let's see if we can sort this out," she said, and opened the folder.

The next little period of time in that room was very quiet. It was so quiet that after a while Meehan realized he was listening to a clock tick in some other room.

In this room, the only sound was the occasional *shrush* when Judge Foote turned over one of the documents to give an equal fish-eye to the next. She was giving a lot of fish-eye. From time to time, she would look up and give Meehan the fish-eye, and he would blink slowly at her, trying for no expression at all, trying in Stanislavski style to recall how he'd done it, at the age of ten, when he was Kneeling Shepherd in that Adoration of the Magi tableau in parochial school. Then Judge Foote would look down again, turn another page, and this time give Goldfarb the fish-eye. Meehan didn't dare turn his head to see how Goldfarb was dealing with it, but he assumed attorneys got the fish-eye all the time and had worked out coping mechanisms.

At last, the final document had been studied and digested— or maybe not digested—and Judge Foote gave them both the fish-eye at once, leaving the folder open on her desk. "Interesting," she said.

Neither of them said anything, while Judge Foote nodded, agreeing with herself. "A lot of signatures here," she commented.

"Everybody's signed off, Your Honor," Goldfarb said, as though she were merely agreeing, but Meehan understood (and so would Your Honor) that a little pressure had just been brought to bear.

Which Judge Foote didn't like; Meehan could see her nose wrinkle, as she smelled something less pleasant than a cooling pie here in her tree-trunk parlor in the woods. "Not quite everybody," she said.

"Well, not you, no, Your Honor," Goldfarb said, and Meehan decided this was why she wasn't off with some big firm, with her brains, making the big bucks; she didn't know how to tread lightly.

"Oh, more than that," Judge Foote said, with a little disdainful wave at the folder. "For instance, I don't have the psychiatric evaluation."

"Oh, I think you do, Your Honor," Goldfarb said, half rising, as though to help the judge paw through the papers, then settling again. "From Dr. Steingutt at the MCC."

"*That's* the psychiatric evaluation?"

"Yes, Your Honor."

"I saw that," Judge Foote said. "Dr. Steingutt writes that he never actually saw the prisoner Meehan."

"No, Your Honor," Goldfarb said, "Dr. Steingutt explains he's based his judgment on the record of Mr. Meehan's behavior while in detention."

"In eleven days of detention," Judge Foote said. "We're giving new meaning to the term 'rush to judgment' here."

"Yes, Your Honor," Goldfarb said, apparently having finally realized her job at the moment was to back off.

The judge's look toward Meehan this time was almost kindly, as though he actually were the wayward twelve-year-old she'd been anticipating. "What is *your* psychiatric evaluation, Mr. Meehan?" she asked him.

He blinked. "I'm sorry? Evaluation, of what?"

"Of you," she told him. "Tell me your psychiatric evaluation of yourself."

Meehan was just on the verge of describing a self based largely on Tom Sawyer when he suddenly recalled one of the most important of the ten thousand rules, which is: Always Tell the Truth. (The codicils to that one are (1) If you can't think of anything else, (2) If it's unexpected, and (3) If it can't hurt you, all of which is because (4) It's easier to remember.)

So he said, "I get along with other people pretty good, but basically I'm the type that's a loner. I'm not a crazy or a child molester. I'm not political or violent. I do whatever I gotta do to keep myself in nuts and berries, but I don't think I'm greedy."

She nodded through this, and kept on nodding when he was finished, then stopped nodding to say, "But you're a criminal."

"Sure," he said.

"Wouldn't you describe yourself as antisocial?"

"Anti?" He was surprised, but not offended; she just didn't understand yet. "I'm not against society," he said. "I need it. Just like you do, or anybody else. I got no objection to society at all. I do try to keep out of its way."

"And what," she asked him, "do you see as your position in society?"

He couldn't resist. Hoping to achieve a boyish grin and a shrug, he said, "Usually, on a fire escape."

She laughed, so it had been a good gamble to take. But then she cocked an eye at him and said, "But not to peek."

"Oh, no," he said. "There wouldn't be time. Besides, leave other people alone, that's my idea."

Goldfarb said, "Your Honor, that's very close to Dr. Steingutt's findings."

"Mmm," the judge said, and said to Meehan, "Francis, did you read Dr. Steingutt's report?"

"Your Honor," he said, "I haven't read or looked at one piece of paper in there. Ms. Goldfarb here, she just takes me from place to place, and I do what she says."

"I see." She leafed through documents briefly, clearly thinking it over, then gave Goldfarb a brand-new fish-eye and said, "There's no home visit here."

Goldfarb began, "Your Honor—"

Judge Foote overrode her: "I cannot complete this hearing

without the results of the home visit. A qualified social worker must visit the home and submit a report on the child's— Well. On the child's home environment. Without that, I don't see how I can proceed."

"Your Honor," Goldfarb said, beginning to sound a little desperate, "in the time frame of this situation, Mr. Mee— Francis's home environment was the Manhattan Correctional Center. None of us would want a qualified social worker's assessment of that environment. Since he was removed from that inappropriate environment, at the request of the district attorney, he has been in my custody. I am a member of the bar and an officer of the court. If you insist on a home visit to my apart—"

Sounding a bit shocked, Judge Foote said, "Is he *living* with you?"

"No, he is not," Goldfarb said, also sounding shocked.

"I'm in the Crowne Royale, it's a hotel in Manhattan," Meehan hastily told her, and pulled the key from his pocket. "Three-eighteen. See?"

"It's a hotel room," Goldfarb said. "There's really not much there for a social worker to evaluate."

"I don't have a river view," Meehan volunteered (though one should never volunteer). "I think if I was on a higher floor, maybe I would."

Judge Foote frowned at the documents. "The people who have already passed this along," she said, looking down at her desk rather than at them, "are supposed to impress me and they do. There's really nothing for me at this point but to add my little bit to the farrago."

Neither Meehan nor Goldfarb said a word. In fact, neither of them breathed.

"I suppose my objecting to minor irregularities in the midst of this monster irregularity," she said, lifting her eyes to him, not looking happy, "merely shows an inability on my part to see the big picture. Do you see the big picture, Francis?"

"Never have, Your Honor," Meehan told her. "I'm lucky if I make sense of the inset."

She smiled; wintry, but a smile. "I'd love to know what this is all about," she said, "but I know better than to ask. All right, Ms. Goldfarb, I will remand Francis Xavier Meehan into your custody."

"Thank you, Your Honor," Goldfarb said.

Judge Foote actually laughed; a hearty laugh, like a contralto. She said, "I think I'm getting into the swing of it. Yes, Ms. Goldfarb, I remand Francis Xavier Meehan into your custody . . . until his eighteenth birthday."

"Thank you, Your Honor," said Goldfarb and Meehan.

# 34

THE LIMO WAS supposed to wait for them, and there it was, in the No Standing Zone in front of the building, the chauffeur at the wheel, reading the *Amsterdam News*, while hundreds of cops, along with lawyers and felons and witnesses and family members and people in bandages, moved in and out of and all around the building. There were no other vehicles stopped anywhere along there, so apparently some cars were more equal than others.

Meehan had been afraid to speak during their journey through the halls and elevator and across the sidewalk, but once they were safely in the limo he said, "Didn't she know anything about the story at *all?*"

"Wait," Goldfarb said. "Let me call Jeffords." And she pulled a little cellphone out of her shoulderbag.

So Meehan waited, and listened to Goldfarb greet Jeffords and tell him everything had worked out okay. Then she moved forward to the rear-facing seats and extended the phone to the chauffeur, saying, "He's going to give you directions to the restaurant."

The chauffeur took the phone, listened, nodded, made

some notes on a pad suction-cupped to the dashboard, and gave the phone back. Then he waited for Goldfarb to come sit beside Meehan again before he started up.

"A little," Goldfarb said.

Meehan looked at her. "A little what?"

"She had been told a little," Goldfarb explained.

"Oh, the judge."

"That's the question you asked me."

"Yeah, I did, I remember that."

"I don't know who talked to her," Goldfarb said, "but she would have been told it was a special case with some oddities in it."

"I *guess.*"

"Before she saw the documents in the case," Goldfarb went on, "and the people who'd already signed off, it would not have been a good idea to tell her the oddity was that the juvenile was forty-two years old."

Meehan grinned. The limo, he noticed, was just passing Atomic Lanes. He said, "She dealt with it pretty good, then."

"I'm sure she's worked in the system a long while," Goldfarb said. "You may be the oddest oddity she's ever come across, but you're not the *only* oddity she's ever been expected to blink at."

Meehan nodded, thinking about that. "Life in the square world," he said, "is more complicated than I thought."


The restaurant was out on Long Island, on the north shore, a spread-out pale room with large north-facing windows that offered a hilltop view of Long Island Sound, with the southern coast of Connecticut far away. The middle of October, and a little too cool for it, but the powerboats still bobbed and batted around out there, undistracted by any serious shipping.

Jeffords was there first and had not only snagged a window-side table but had grabbed for himself the best seat for

looking out at the view. He stood from it to greet them, shook
Goldfarb's hand, hesitated, then pretended he hadn't hesitated
as he enthusiastically shook Meehan's hand, saying, "So you're
a free man."

"With a leash," Meehan said. "Goldfarb tells me I have a
leash."

"Oh, I wouldn't worry about it," Jeffords said. "Sit down, sit
down."

Meehan gave Goldfarb the second-best seat and took for
himself the chair at right angles to the view. He could have a
conversation, or he could look out at the water, as it winked
sunlight here and there off its little wavelets.

Jeffords and Goldfarb wanted to have their own conversation, about the law and what had been done and how it had
worked out, so Meehan watched the boats and the waves until
after they'd ordered various kinds of seafood and one kind of
white wine. Then Jeffords turned to him and said, "That leash
is gonna come off you by Thursday, I know it is, so there's
nothing to worry about."

"Tomorrow," Meehan said. "Expect a phone call."

"No details!" Goldfarb said.

"That's wonderful," Jeffords told him. "I knew, Francis, the
minute I saw you in the MCC, I knew you were our man."

"I haven't heard from Yehudi and Mostafa any more," Meehan said, "but I do keep wondering about them. I don't want
them to suddenly show up, making heavy noises while I'm trying to work."

"Something else not to worry about," Jeffords assured him.
"That's the other thing I wanted to tell you. That has been totally resolved, forever."

"Good," Meehan said.

"The president himself got involved," Jeffords said. "We
didn't want him to have to, and *he* certainly didn't want to have

to, but our friend Arthur, when he talked to those foreign intelligence people, he opened a real Pandora's box."

"I'm sure he did," Meehan said.

"So that's why the president himself had to intervene."

Meehan said, "With Israel and Egypt?"

"No no no, with Arthur. The president can't acknowledge any of this to our allies."

Meehan wasn't so sure of this. He said, "But you think he's got Arthur to shut Pandora down again."

"Absolutely." Jeffords paused to taste and approve the wine, then said, "The president gave Arthur the ultimate threat, from his own lips."

Meehan thought, Wow. From a president, that might be scary. He said, "The ultimate threat?"

"That's right." Jeffords leaned forward, and lowered his voice. "The president told Arthur, one more appearance by those people, of any kind, and Arthur is delisted from the White House inaugural ball."

Meehan looked at him. Jeffords lifted his glass, beaming at them both. "To crime," the smug jerk said.

# 35

ONE THOUGHT LEADS to another, or there's an association of ideas, or this leads to that. Whatever; in the limo, headed back toward Manhattan, Meehan found himself thinking about the limo they were going to need tomorrow. Obviously they'd have to boost one, but from where? By the time it got to Burnstone it would have to carry Massachusetts plates, but that could happen anywhere along the line. The main point was, where to pick up a limo. It's not like an ordinary car, you don't often see one parked by itself just somewhere along the curb.

He thought, should I ask the driver where this one's stored? What reason would I have? Nothing good, and everybody would know it.

Goldfarb broke into his reflections, then, saying, "In a funny way, I'm gonna miss you, Meehan."

He looked at her, not getting it. "What?"

She gazed out her window at the borough going by. "Though I suppose, really," she told the view, "what I'll miss is not going to the MCC."

He said, "Goldfarb? What are you talking about?"

Now she did look at him, seeming a bit surprised. "*You're*

out of the MCC, Meehan," she said, "but *I'm* not. I'm serving a life sentence in that place."

"Oh," he said, "you're talking about the MCC."

"What else did you think I was talking about? I still have to make a living."

"I thought you were talking about us," he said.

She lowered her head, the better to eyeball him through her big glasses. "What us?"

So he thought about it, looking first at the back of the chauffeur's head, way up there, and then at his own knees, and finally at the face of Goldfarb, which gave him nothing back. "You are talking about us," he said. "You're saying goodbye."

"I'm your lawyer, Meehan," she pointed out. "The case is over. We went before the judge, and you're a free man."

"In your custody."

"That's a technicality," she said.

"In my experience," he told her, "it's the technicalities that clothesline you."

She frowned at him. "Do what?"

"Clothesline," he repeated. "It's from football, if you're running and a guy sticks his arm out straight to the side so your neck runs into his arm, that's clothesline. You don't see it coming, and it can do damage. In football, it's illegal."

"Why do they call it clothesline?"

"I dunno."

She sat back, and he could see she was thinking on it. She said, "If you don't use a clothes dryer, you hang your stuff out on the line."

"Not in the city."

"No," she agreed. "Upstate. But let's say you were upstate, and you were committing a burglary."

"I'm rehabilitated," he said.

"Almost," she told him. "And let's say the homeowner came home, and chased you."

Similar things had indeed occurred. "Uh-huh," Meehan said.

"So you're running down the backyards," she went on, "looking over your shoulder to see if he's catching up, and you don't see that clothesline in front of you."

"Ow," he said, putting a protective hand to his throat. "That could take your head off."

"I bet that's where it comes from," she said. "Clothesline."

"Yeah, maybe so," he said, caressing his throat.

She nodded. "I love phrases from before technology," she said. "That we still use."

"Uh-huh," he said. "Listen, I don't want to say goodbye."

She looked at him. "Why not?"

"I dunno," he said. "I got used to talking with you. Clothesline and all that. You know, I think when I saw you that time in your apartment with the gun in your hand, stalking those guys, I decided I liked you. You're kinda goofy and fun."

"Thanks a lot," she said.

"But if you don't see any point in being around *me* any more," he said, "then obviously forget it."

"I was brought in as your lawyer," she reminded him.

"By me."

"And I'm grateful. It's been fun."

"But now it's over," he said.

"You don't need a lawyer any more. I *hope* you don't need a lawyer any more."

"I get it," he said.

He looked at the chauffeur and tried to think about needing a limo tomorrow. After a few minutes, he actually was thinking about needing that limo tomorrow, and thinking the thing to do might be go up to Massachusetts tonight with Bernie, find a limo company in the yellow pages, see what was what.

"Meehan," she said.

He looked at her. "Yeah?"

Her face was wrinkled into a very complicated frown. "Were you hitting on me?"

"What? You can't hit on your lawyer, that isn't one— That isn't done." He'd almost said something about the ten thousand rules, which would have been a very stupid thing to do.

"I'm not your lawyer any more," she pointed out. "Not since we came out of Judge Foote's chambers."

"Oh, yeah?" He gave her a happy grin. "Then I *can* hit on you!"

She sat there watching him, not saying anything, until he became uncertain. "Goldfarb," he said, "you've got me insecure."

"I have?"

"I'm not usually insecure," he told her.

"I've noticed that," she said.

He nodded, thinking it over, then said, "I tell you what. Let's swing around my hotel first, let me pick up a couple things, then I'll come up to your place with you, I mean, your place is also your office—"

"It is."

"—and we can discuss it," he said. "Clear the air."

"That's a good idea," she said. "I think we ought to clear the air."

"Good."

"I don't want you insecure," she said.

Damn if the red light on the phone wasn't blinking *again!* He almost didn't answer it, having other things on his mind, but then he did, and it was Jeffords, and he sounded awful. Whispering, gulping, hurried, terrified: "Francis, for God's sake, call me! Call me as soon as you can!"

So he did, and Jeffords answered on the first ring, sound-

ing even worse: *"What?"* A ragged but loud shrill whisper, right
next to the phone.

"I can hear you," Meehan said. "Take it easy."

"Francis! Thank God! Come get me, Francis! Come get me
out of here!"

"Get you out of where? What happened to you?"

"They kidnapped me! Quick, come get me!"

Then Meehan got it: "What, Yehudi and Mostafa?"

"I don't *know* who they are, I only want—"

"So much for your president and his ultimate threat."

*"Don't* lord it over me now, Francis, I'm in desperate trouble! They're going to cut my fingers off!"

"Who is? Why?"

*"These people!* If I don't tell them where you are and what
you're after!"

"All right," Meehan said. "Run it by me once, beginning to
end, and I'll see what I can do."

Jeffords gulped, made a strangled sound, then said, "Right
after lunch, in the restaurant parking lot, they grabbed me,
threw me in a delivery van, held a gun on me, drove me here,
said they're waiting for their expert to come up from DC, *he's*
the one cuts the fingers off, if I don't tell them before he gets
here he'll cut one finger off an hour, and then one toe, and
then the ears. I don't know what he does after the ears."

"I doubt the question ever comes up," Meehan said. "So
where are you?"

"Upper West Side, off Broadway. I could see Broadway
down the street when they took me out of the van, there's a
Sloan's supermarket on the corner, I'm in a little building,
there's a red neon sign READER in the front window, they
shoved me down in the basement here, some kind of storage
room, it's *very dark*, they took my wallet and my watch but I
hid the phone in my sock when I was in the van, and I have

it on vibrate so it won't ring, and you're the only one I can think of—"

"Cops," Meehan advised.

"No!"

"Dial 911," Meehan suggested.

"It'll go public! It'll all go public!"

"You'll have all your fingers."

"But I won't have a job, ever again. I won't have an entire *administration!* Do you want to see the Other Side in the White House? Do you know what a disaster that would be?"

"Actually, I don't," Meehan said.

"Come get me, Francis," Jeffords begged. "I'm begging you."

"Change of plans," Meehan said, as he got into the limo.

Goldfarb gave him a fish-eye Judge Foote would have been proud of. "Oh, yeah?"

"Jeffords on the answering machine. I called him, and Yehudi and Mostafa kidnapped him, they're waiting for a specialist to come cut his fingers off if he doesn't talk about me and the package. He won't call the cops, so I gotta go rescue him."

"You have to rescue Pat Jeffords," she said, in an extremely flat way.

"That's the story," he said, and shrugged, because that was the story.

She thought about it, then shook her head. "There have to be easier ways to avoid commitment."

"And I know all of them," he assured her. "They've got him in a building up in your neighborhood, in a place with a Reader, you know, one of those Gypsy psychics, down the block from a Sloan's."

"There's a couple of Sloan's up there," she said, still frowning very hard.

"Well, he's near one of them."

"I'll come with you," she said.

"Don't be crazy," he told her.

"I'm not," she said, and called to the chauffeur, "We want to go up Broadway."

He saluted in the mirror, and started them away from the curb. She turned back to Meehan: "You carrying?"

"Carrying what?"

"Heat!" she exclaimed. "A rod! A gat!"

"I never carry a gun," he said.

"Well, I do," she said. "We'll go to my place first." Leaning forward again, she called to the chauffeur, "Never mind Broadway, we'll go back to where you picked me up," and the chauffeur saluted in the mirror again.

They rolled northward, and Meehan said, "Jeffords'll like this, being rescued by a lawyer in a limo."

Aᴛᴛᴇʀ Gᴏʟᴅꜰᴀʀʙ ᴡᴇɴᴛ into her building, Meehan moved to the rear-facing seat, up by the chauffeur, and said, "This is really a nice clean car you got here."

The chauffeur, surprised but amiable, smiled at him in the mirror and said, "Yes, it is. Thanks."

"You keep it in a garage?"

The chauffeur grinned, shaking his head. "It's not *my* car," he said, "belongs to a big outfit up in the Bronx."

"Oh."

"They got everything," he said. "They got buses and vans and limos and even ambulances."

"Big outfit," Meehan guessed.

"You know it," the chauffeur said. "But no garages, just the one big lot."

"Thinka that," Meehan said.

"The limos," the chauffeur told him, "get run through the car wash every time they go out on a job. The rest of the time, they're just in there with everything else, the buses and the vans and the Dobermans."

"Ambulances, you said."

"Right, ambulances, too," the chauffeur agreed.

Meehan said, "Dobermans?"

"You got graffiti kids up there," the chauffeur explained. "If they didn't have all those Dobermans on the lot, those kids'd crawl over the fence, they don't even *care* about razor wire, they'd be in there spray-painting initials over everything in sight. Even a nice limo like this," he said. "They got no respect at all, those kids."

"Dobermans," Meehan said.

"They sure keep those kids out," the chauffeur said, "you can bet on that."

"I'm sure they do," Meehan said, and when Goldfarb came out of her building, clutching her big bag close to her side, Meehan was back in his own seat, brooding out at the traffic, thinking about limos. Limos without Dobermans.

The chauffeur hopped out to open Goldfarb's door, and she got in, giving Meehan a meaningful look as she patted her bag. Now she was carrying.

The chauffeur returned behind the wheel of this un-obtainable limo and Goldfarb called to him, "Now we want to cruise Broadway, kind of slow. We're looking for a Sloan's."

The chauffeur said, "Uptown or downtown?"

They looked at one another, and Meehan called, "We'll go downtown first. If we don't find anything by Seventy-second, we'll come back up."

"Done," the chauffeur said, and did his mirror salute.

As they started across toward Broadway, Goldfarb said, "You didn't get your stuff from your room."

"Jeffords distracted me," he said. "I'll get it later."

"Jeffords," she said. "That's unbelievable, to kidnap a man in broad daylight."

"Where they're from," Meehan said, "I think that's standard

operating procedure. You kidnap somebody, that's the way you start a dialogue."

"I'll stick to the phone," she said.

They found a wrong Sloan's in the 70s, with no Reader nearby, and the right Sloan's in the 90s. Down the block from the Reader was a fire hydrant, beside which the chauffeur stopped the car.

"We won't be long," Goldfarb told him, which Meehan hoped was right, and they walked back to the building, one of a row of narrow four-story brick places, this the only one with a shop front on the ground floor. Tarot symbols and dolls and globes and a sleeping cat were in the display window, along with the narrow-lettered red neon READER sign suspended behind the glass, all framed by what looked like a shower curtain with moons and stars painted on it swagged open. Beyond the window was a small empty living room, pale little furniture on light green industrial carpet, crucifixes and other religious ornamentation on the wall, and beside the window was the door, which was locked and bore a sign RING BELL under the hand-painted golden MADAME SYLVIA.

"I'll step to one side," Meehan said. "They won't realize you're the dangerous one."

"They will soon," she said, and pushed the button.

Meehan had thought the bell would be answered by Madame Sylvia, but when he slid through the widening space behind Goldfarb what he looked at was very unlikely to be called either Madame *or* Sylvia. This was a bulky guy, hairy shoulders revealed by his dirty white strap undershirt above shapeless dark blue work pants and black work boots. He wore rings and bracelets and a watch and various tattoos, and he'd started to say, "Madame Sylvia will—" when he saw Meehan come in, and went into hostile mode: "What's this?"

"Show him the rod, sugar," Meehan said, elbowing the door shut behind him.

"Victor!" the guy yelled at the curtained doorway behind him, but then he backed away as Goldfarb unpacked the iron. "What's goin on?"

As Victor, a slightly uglier version of the first one, but in a T-shirt that advertised beer, came pushing through the curtain, and as Goldfarb gripped the pistol in her right hand, resting its butt on the cupped palm of her left hand to show she'd taken some lessons somewhere, not quite pointing the barrel at any-body, Meehan reached into her big bag hanging from her left shoulder and muttered, "Your cellphone."

Victor and the first one asked each other questions in a language all their own, while Meehan pulled out the cellphone and punched in Jeffords' number. He had to be fast before they agreed on a counterattack, which they would definitely do once they got over the first shock.

"*Hello?*" Still terrified.

"Jeffords!" Meehan yelled, a name that made Victor and his friend stop talking to stare wide-eyed. "Hang up, switch your phone to ring, and I'll call you back." He broke the connection, said to the two guys, "Listen for the ring," punched redial, and they all heard the faint faraway ding-a-ling in the basement.

"*Hello!*"

"Jeffords," Meehan said, "if you hear any trouble up here, or this phone hangs up, dial 911 right *then* and we'll figure it out later. You got me?"

"Where are you?"

"We're upstairs, you idiot, where do you think we are?" Pointing his free hand at Victor, he said, "Go down and let him out, or we fill the place with cops."

The two guys babbled together, and a woman in a scarlet ball gown and gold turban came through the curtain, carrying an ax. Now all three babbled together.

Meehan said, "Goldfarb, can you shoot that picture of Satan over there on the wall?"

"Is *that* what that ugly thing is?" she said, and shot it in the belly. The *clap* ricocheted around the room. Glass from the frame spattered all over the place, and three barefoot children ran through the curtain, screaming. They immediately switched over to loud crying, while the woman with the ax told them to shut up and Meehan yelled at Victor, "Get down there now before the elephants show up!"

"We got a guy comin," Victor said, "explain everything."

"The guy from DC, to cut off his fingers," Meehan said, and Jeffords on the cellphone moaned. "I know all about him, we'll take a raincheck. What do you want, Victor? Right now, this second, you let him go, or we fill the place with cops."

The woman with the ax yelled at Goldfarb, who responded by pointing the pistol directly at her forehead. The woman sneered. "You wouldn't shoot nobody."

"She's a lawyer, lady," Meehan told her, "she's capable of anything." Then, into the phone, since nobody was moving, he yelled, "All right, screw it, Jeffords, they aren't going to release you, we'll both hang up, we'll both call 911, we don't want to be here—"

"Wait!" It was Victor, at last getting the idea, holding his hands out as though to stop a stampede. "I'll get him! I'll get him!"

"Victor's coming to get you," Meehan told the phone. "Don't hang up, I wanna hear everything that happens."

Victor left, and the woman pointed her ax at the shot picture. "That was an antique," she said. "You gotta pay for that."

"Send me a bill," Goldfarb told her.

"I could take you to small-claims court."

"I wish you would," Goldfarb said. "What a nice list of witnesses we could have."

The woman looked sulky. "I bet you are a lawyer," she

said, and Jeffords hurtled into the room, his own cellphone to his ear, his face and clothing streaked with dirt. *"I'm here!"* he yelled into his phone and into Meehan's ear, and Meehan recoiled, shouting, *"Jee-*zis, moderate it, will ya?"

"Out," Goldfarb said to Jeffords, keeping both hands on the gun, nodding her head backward at the door, as Victor reappeared. Meehan opened the door, and Jeffords exited at a dead run, Meehan telling him, "Hang a left," as he tore by. Then Meehan followed, and Goldfarb backed out last, the men and the woman with the ax glaring, the three kids having tantrums.

Goldfarb slid the gun into her bag as she and Meehan hurried after Jeffords, who would have shot right on by their wheels if Meehan hadn't yelled, "The limo!" Jeffords turned on a dime, yanked open the limo door, and hurled himself in headfirst.

Goldfarb and Meehan followed, more sanely, and when Meehan looked back, there was a taxi pulling up at Reader, and Victor and the other guy were running out to the sidewalk, both pointing toward the limo.

"Back to the hotel," Meehan called to the chauffeur, as he pulled the door shut.

Goldfarb was in her usual seat, with Jeffords on the floor, scrambling around. Meehan took his own seat and saw the discussion continue back there, two new ones having climbed out of the cab. "Your doctors just arrived," he said.

The traffic light at the corner being miraculously green, the limo took the left onto West End. Jeffords sorted himself out, and climbed onto the rear-facing seat, then said, "Why the hotel?"

"Because they haven't found me yet," Meehan told him. "So it's safe." To Goldfarb he said, "Your place isn't."

"God *damn* it," she said. "I have to check in there again?"

"I will, too," Jeffords said. "They have my wallet, they know my address, I don't dare go home. In fact," to Goldfarb, "I'm going to have to ask you to sign for my room. You'll get it back."

Meehan said, "What are you gonna do about your wallet?"

"Call Arthur," said Jeffords. With grim satisfaction, he said, "And I shall tell him that his access to the president is history. *And* I want my wallet *and* my watch back from those friends of his. And there's a certain History of Steam museum," he went on, with savage gusto now that he wasn't being held by the bad guys any more, "in some certain someone's congressional district, that is *very* unlikely to be constructed after all."

# 37

OF COURSE THE red light was winking on the telephone, but it could possibly be either Goldfarb or Jeffords, both of whom he'd left in the lobby, checking in. But could they have gotten to their rooms this fast?

No. Bernie's voice: "We've got the truck. Bob and I'll drive up in the morning, let me know where and when we meet. And how you doing with the limo?"

"I'll get back to you on that," Meehan told the dead phone, capped it, and when it rang again eight minutes later he was actually in the room to pick up the receiver and say, "Here."

It was Goldfarb: "You know it's time for lunch."

Surprised, he looked at the bedside clock, and it told him 2:13. Eleven this morning the meeting with Judge Foote, then home, then running around rescuing Jeffords from the pedicurists, and now it was after two. Meehan's stomach growled, for confirmation. "We should do something about that," he said.

She said, "With Jeffords or without?"

There were things to talk about with Jeffords. "I tell you what," Meehan said. "Lunch with, dinner without."

"Smart," she said.

\*     \*     \*

Jeffords chose the place, a Greek diner tucked into the bottom corner of an old stone apartment building a couple blocks north of the Crowne Royale. They sat in a pale blue vinyl-and-chrome booth with a pale blue Formica table and read a menu sixty-four pages long, at the end of which Goldfarb told the Vietnamese waiter she wanted the Greek salad with feta cheese, Jeffords wanted the feta cheese omelet, and Meehan wanted a hamburger with everything and french fries. The waiter sloped away and Goldfarb told Meehan, "That isn't healthy."

"I know," he agreed. "Everything they give you in the MCC is healthy. It's crap, but it's healthy crap. My destiny was, I was gonna eat healthy crap and keep regular hours the rest of my life."

"Enjoy," she decided.

"You know it."

Jeffords said, "I thought *my* destiny was to be shish kebab." Now that his ordeal and the escape therefrom were over, and he'd cleaned himself up as best he could with no change of clothing, he no longer looked so much terrified as worn down by a long-term but not quite terminal disease. His eyes were wide, and shadowed all around with light gray, like dustings from a tombstone. His lips were pale, mouth wider than before in an unconscious rictus, and twitching from time to time. The tops of his ears seemed to lean closer to his head. His hands moved constantly, and Meehan didn't look forward to watching him try to eat an omelet.

To calm him, if possible, Meehan said, "Well, it's over."

"I don't know about that," Jeffords said. "I had to make contact with Bruce, of course, tell Bruce to get the word to the president and to stomp on Arthur hard, because everybody in DC"—lowering his voice, looking guiltily around like a conspirator in a silent movie—"is *very worried* about this situation.

This could blow up in everybody's faces, this could be worse than Watergate, worse than Iran-Contra, worse than the little blue dress."

Meehan said, "You people kinda *specialize* in farce down there in DC, don't you?"

"Not on purpose," Jeffords said.

"No, I didn't say you did anything on purpose, down there in DC," Meehan agreed. "But when you say everybody in DC is worried about this operation, just how many people is everybody? How many people are looking over my shoulder here? The Joint Chiefs of Staff? The attorney general? The *surgeon* general?"

"No, not at all," Jeffords said, "of course not. At this point, it's still only the president's inner circle—"

"A hundred thousand big mouths," Meehan suggested.

"Certainly not," Jeffords said. "A small tight group of people, absolutely loyal to the president."

"Does this group include your friend Arthur?"

Jeffords' lips pursed. "The rotten apple in the barrel. Bruce is taking care of that, he tells me Arthur could not be more abashed—"

"I bet *I* could make him more abashed."

"Possibly. But without you, no, he could not be more abashed. My wallet and watch will be delivered this afternoon."

Meehan sat up straighter. "Delivered where?"

"I'm not an idiot, Meehan," Jeffords alleged. "It's being delivered to our Manhattan campaign headquarters."

"And how do you pick it up?"

"After lunch, I'll phone a trusted friend—"

"More trust."

Jeffords said, "There has to be trust *somewhere*, Francis."

Meehan nodded. "How you people don't all wind up in the MCC, I'll never know."

"Life is unfair," Goldfarb informed him. "A president said that."

"He would know," Meehan agreed.

Goldfarb said, "Excuse me, gentlemen, the powder room calls," and got to her feet.

This had been prearranged between Goldfarb and Meehan, since she was dead-set against learning any of what she called "details," some of which Meehan would have to go over with Jeffords at this lunch; besides which, she probably had to go. Anyway, she went, and Meehan said, "Let me change the subject."

"I wish you would," Jeffords said. "I'll just say, I *will* get my wallet and watch returned without compromising our operation."

"Compromising our operation," Meehan echoed. "I like that."

"I know, as Bruce and I agreed at the beginning of all this," Jeffords said, "that we needed to bring in a professional, but I now see that the downside of bringing in a professional is that he comes with the professional's insufferable arrogance."

Meehan said, "Would you rather go back and hang out with Reader?"

"Of course not."

"Okay, then. Let me tell you what we've got to do now. You wanted to be part of the heist in the first place, and I said no—"

"More insufferable arrogance, as I recall," Jeffords said. "Thirty-five dollars an hour if I watch, forty-five if I help."

"Oh, good, you remembered," Meehan said. "But now the situation's different. You're the one guy they can get at who knows *where* the heist goes down. I can't have you wandering around loose, deciding who you trust."

The food arrived then, and Jeffords' lips remained pursed

throughout the delivery, unpursing when they were once again alone, saying, "What are you suggesting?"

"You come along," Meehan told him. "Tomorrow morning, early. We gotta leave here at seven."

"That *is* early."

"Crime never sleeps," Meehan said.

Jeffords frowned. "I thought that was rust."

"It was. Here's the other thing. By seven in the morning, I need you to have us a limo."

Jeffords blinked. "A limo?"

"Like the one we were in today," Meehan explained. "I don't know if you rent it, or what. But without a driver."

"Why? Who's going to be the driver?"

"First me, then somebody else," Meehan told him. "Never you."

"There you go again," Jeffords said.

Meehan said, "Tell me you can get me this limo."

"Of course I can get you the limo," Jeffords said, showing a trace of his own insufferable arrogance. "The Manhattan campaign office has several vehicles on loan or lease, including I believe two limousines. They usually have drivers assigned, but I could certainly sign one out for myself."

"Do," Meehan told him. "Have them deliver it to the hotel at seven tomorrow morning. They can bring you your watch and wallet at the same time."

"Good idea," Jeffords said, nodding, then all at once he frowned and said, "Will this vehicle be used in the burglary?"

"Of course," Meehan told him.

Jeffords agonized, was torn. "I *am* getting deeper into this," he said. "It sucks you in, you can't help yourself."

"You have to help yourself to some extent," Meehan told him. "I've got to bring you along, I got no choice there, but when we're on the job you just do what I say and stay out of the way. Don't help, don't argue, don't ask questions. Just pretend you aren't there, because God knows I don't want you there."

"I understand," Jeffords said, and looked bitter. "This is all Arthur's fault," he said.

Meehan said, "Because we were on his plane, and a guy named Howie was on the plane that you didn't know was gonna be there, and he had a curious nose and a big mouth."

Jeffords looked at him. "You mean it's all *my* fault," he said.

"I mean," Meehan told him, "there's fault enough to go around," and Goldfarb came back and said, "Oh, good. Food."

They ate awhile, and then Jeffords said, "I'll have to find us a different kind of place for dinner."

Goldfarb looked at Meehan, who said to Jeffords, "Goldfarb and I have an appointment for dinner, we gotta do some lawyer-client stuff."

Jeffords looked bewildered. "Lawyer-client? But didn't you finish all that?"

Goldfarb said, "There's always final particulars, a case like this, things to be wrapped up."

"Well . . ." Jeffords was lost. "What do I do tonight?"

"Watch television," Goldfarb suggested.

"Eat in," Meehan told him. "You don't want to show yourself on the street."

Jeffords looked stricken.

Meehan said, "Besides, you've got to get up early."

Which brightened Jeffords up a little, the prospect of tomorrow. "That's right," he said, and told Goldfarb, "We're leaving at seven in the morning."

She reared back, wide-eyed. "Was that a detail?"

"Nah," Meehan said.

THIS TIME, THEY chose a little old-fashioned French restaurant in the West Forties, walking distance from the Crowne Royale, the kind of place that features coq au vin on the menu and red-and-white check cloths on the tables. They ordered some stuff, including red wine, and clinked glasses, and then she said, "Let me tell you the problem, right up front."

"I'm the problem," Meehan said.

"Truer words were never spoken." Looking at the wine in her glass, the glass on the red-and-white check cloth, she said, "I've seen your dossier, you know."

"Sure, you're my lawyer."

"There's nothing much hopeful in there," she told him. "In fact, it's all mostly hopeless."

"Uh-huh."

"You're a recidivist," she said, "you're an autodidact, no degrees, no marketable—"

"Wait a second," he said. "What was that one? The second one. I know recidivist, that's what's going on my tombstone, Francis Xavier Meehan, Recidivist. But what was the other?"

She grinned at him. "That's funny," she said. "The one word

every autodidact doesn't know is autodidact. It means self-taught."

"Self-taught."

"You dropped out of high school, but you're a reader, and you've picked up a lot of stuff. And, given the amount of time you've spent behind bars," she added drily, "you've had plenty of time for reading."

"A little more than absolutely necessary," he said.

"If your country hadn't called you," she said, "you'd have nothing but reading time for the rest of your life."

"We call that a close call," he said.

"No," she told him, "we call it deus ex machina."

"I know that one," he said. "God from the machine, the way they'd end the old Greek plays."

"A miracle, in other words," she summed up. "So here you are out, doing what you do. The way the drummer boy drummed his drum for the infant baby Jesus, you burgle for the USA."

"For my president," he corrected. "Whoever he is."

"And the question is," she said, "once you've done this patriotic breaking and entering, what then? Do you even know where the straight and narrow *is?*"

He felt awful about this, and said so: "I feel awful about this. I don't know what else I'm gonna do. There'll be a little profit out of tomorrow's event—"

"No details!"

"No details," he agreed. "But then what? I sit around the house, or wherever I am, and after a while I'm bored, and somebody I know calls me and says, 'I happen to know there's a load of eight BMWs on a truck in New Jersey with nobody watching it, wanna come along?' And I reach for my hat. I mean, that's true, that's who I am."

"And yet," she said, "you were married once, you at least *thought* you were gonna settle down."

"You don't think when you get married," he told her, "or you wouldn't do it. I didn't know so much who I was then, that's all. It lasted three years, and when Barbara threw me out I was ready to go. Not because there was anything wrong with *her*, she was fine, she and her next husband are great together."

"You never see your children—"

"That's my gift to them," he said. "And to myself, to be honest. If I showed up every once in a while, say, with some dumb little gift, hang out for a weekend, then some day I get sent up for five to fifteen, then what? The only pleasure I can give my kids is stay out of their way. They're fifteen and thirteen now, and when they're in their twenties, if I'm out and about, I'll give them a call, we can have a reunion. Up to this point, I could only be trouble for everybody concerned. Way back when we split, I talked this all over with Barbara, and it was mostly her idea, but I had to say then, and I still do, she was right."

"Not such a great solution," she said.

"I agree," he said. "But there we are. And now we come to you, and here you've got the advantage on me, because I *don't* have a dossier that says on the tab, Elaine Goldfarb."

"Okay," she said. "What do you want to know?"

"You're not married now."

"No."

"Were you ever?"

"I was engaged once," she said.

"Oh oh. He didn't leave you at the altar or something, did he?"

"No, it all just sort of faded out," she said. "We were in law school together, we talked about our classes a lot, we helped each other with the work—"

"You helped him more, I bet."

"No, Doug is very smart," she said. "He's in one of the big

corporate New York firms right now, he's married for . . . I think the second time, maybe the third, he's got kids."

"How come *you* aren't in a big corporate New York firm?"

She looked at him over her wineglass. "Can you see me in one of those places?"

"No," he said honestly. "So the question is, what's wrong with you? We know what's wrong with me. What's wrong with you?"

"I'm not sure I approve of that question," she said.

"That's okay," he said. "We don't want the food to get cold, it's very good stuff, we can eat awhile, you think it over."

"Hmmmmm," she said.

So they ate awhile, and decided not to have another bottle of wine, not to have dessert or coffee, and not to have any more conversation in the restaurant. Walking back toward the hotel, she said, "I didn't answer your question."

"I noticed."

"Well, it can wait, anyway," she said. "I mean, we can defer it."

"Oh, yeah?"

"What I'm saying is," she said, looking where she was walking and not looking at him, "and this is awkward for me, but you are not coming to my room tonight, and I am not coming to yours. So we don't have to make any decisions yet."

"How come?" he said.

Shaking her head, speaking as though it should be obvious, she said, "Not with Jeffords under the same roof."

"What?" he said. "It's a *hotel*, it isn't a house or something."

"I don't care, it just wouldn't feel right," she said. "Not with Jeffords there."

"I get it," he said. "We avoid the decision."

She gave him a sharp look. "And *I* get it," she said. "You've decided, that's what's wrong with her."

"Well, it starts the list," he said.

# 39

THE RED LIGHT wasn't blinking on the phone, but that was all right; they were already in the room. Two guys, in the uncomfortable chairs to either side of the oval table by the window. The one writing in a notepad on the table wore a plaid bowtie, blue button-down shirt buttoned down, tan sports jacket, tan chinos, speckle-framed eyeglasses, and receding hair-colored hair. The one leaning back, legs straight out, ankles crossed as he gazed meditatively at the ceiling, wore black tassel loafers, designer blue jeans with a crease, dark gray sports jacket, black turtleneck shirt, Josef Stalin's moustache, and Josef Stalin's hair. Both smiled when Meehan entered the room, and got to their feet. In an amiable, welcoming way, Bowtie said, "Mr. Meehan."

There were so many conflicting signals coming off these guys that Meehan, try as he might, could not find a thing in the ten thousand rules to guide him here. Smiling? But in the room? But a *bowtie?*

They continued to smile at him, Moustache stepping to the side, offering the chair he'd been in, saying, "Have a seat."

Then the appropriate rule did at last surface in his brain: If you don't understand where you are, go somewhere else. "I'll be back in five minutes," he told them, "after you guys leave."

They both raised objections, urging him to stay, but since neither flashed a firearm and one of them did wear a bowtie, Meehan ignored them, left the room, went down to the lobby, found the house phone, called Jeffords' room, and got goddam voice mail. "Goddam it," he told it, "I told you to stay in tonight. I got two guys in my room, I need to know who they are."

He hung up, went over to one of the two skimpy sofas in the lobby's seating area, sat in the one where he could look across the other one toward the street, and tried to figure out who the players were, without a scorecard. Not cops, definitely. Not linked to Yehudi and Mostafa, just as definitely. Not menacing, but on the other hand untroubled by breaking into somebody else's hotel room.

Well, but, they didn't actually *break* in, did they? If they had, Meehan would have noticed scars on the door. So they used some sort of key. Did they walk around with universal keys, or bribe a desk clerk, or what?

Were they from the Other Side, the crowd that wanted to replace the present president with their own president, so Clendon Burnstone IV could get some private bill through Congress? They had the right bland look, but that still didn't seem to explain them.

And here they came, out of the elevator, talking earnestly at one another, then *beaming* with pleasure when they saw Meehan, veering to move straight toward him.

And he got it. Standing, pointing at the belly beneath the bowtie, he said, "Press."

"Yes, of course," said Bowtie.

"We *tried* to identify ourselves," said Moustache, "but you simply turned around and left." With which, he and Bowtie extended business cards, which Meehan took without looking at, but kept in his right hand.

"We understand," Bowtie said soothingly, "that you were startled by our appearance in your room, but we meant nothing threatening at all, I assure you."

Meehan already knew that much. And that they would pull a stunt like that on him meant they knew his background, knew he was one of the people they could walk on. He said, "Get it over with."

Moustache gestured to the sofas. "Shall we sit? Unless you'd rather we talked up in your room."

"I wouldn't rather we talked anywhere," Meehan said. "I'd rather you got to it and got it over with." He almost said, "because I have to get up early," but he didn't want them to know that, did he?

"Well, at least we can get comfortable," Bowtie said. "And we promise not to take up more than a few minutes of your time."

Moustache did his hospitable wave at the sofas again, so Meehan sat back down where he'd been, and they took the sofa facing him over the square Formica coffee table.

Bowtie pulled a little machine from his jacket pocket, saying, "Mind if I tape this?"

"Yes," Meehan said.

Bowtie seemed surprised, but then shrugged, put the machine away, pulled out his notepad instead, and said, "Well, I'll just take notes, then."

"No," Meehan said.

Now Bowtie was truly surprised. "You don't want me to take notes?"

"No."

Moustache said, "Mr. Meehan, an accurate record is to your advantage."

"No, it isn't," Meehan said. "No record at all is to my advantage. What do you want?"

They looked at one another, both shrugged, and Moustache took over, saying, "Essentially, all we want from you is confirmation of a rumor."

Meehan was about to tell him what he could do with his rumor when, over their shoulders, through the street entrance, he saw Jeffords coming in.

Would they know Jeffords by sight? Why not, he was part of the Campaign Committee. To keep these two concentrated on him, and to give Jeffords a chance to get the hell out of sight, Meehan said, "Well, I'll listen. I don't promise anything."

"Of course not," Moustache said. He and Bowtie had little smiles on their faces at all times, as though they knew just a tiny bit more than anybody else in the world and really got a kick out of being who they were.

Halfway across the lobby, Jeffords saw the trio on the sofas, and recoiled like a kitten from a snake. His wide-eyed expression fastened on Meehan as though to say, "How *could* you betray me like this?" while Meehan did his best to keep his own concentration fixed on Moustache and Bowtie.

"The rumor is," Moustache was saying, "that the CC is planning some sort of dirty trick against the challenger, some October Surprise, and that you were plucked from a federal penitentiary to be a part of it."

Yeah, that was the press, in a nutshell. Get everything almost right, but nothing actually *right* at all. It was the Other Side that planned the October Surprise, and the MCC wasn't a federal penitentiary. But it was close enough to do the job, right?

While Jeffords, across the way, finally realized he should stop semaphoring betrayal and start scampering for the elevators, Meehan said, "I think you must have me confused with some other Francis Xavier Meehan. I have absolutely no federal convictions anywhere, you could look that up, and they wouldn't put me in a federal can unless they convicted me of a federal crime, like making war on Portugal or mailing a letter without a stamp."

Bowtie, smirk undiminished, said, "Mr. Meehan, are you going to claim you have *not* been at meetings with Bruce Benjamin and Pat Jeffords of the CC?"

"Sure I saw them," Meehan said. (Jeffords jittered, way over there, in front of a closed elevator door.) "The truth is, I used to live a life of crime, some little while ago, but now I'm rehabilitated, and I'm doing job interviews. Benjamin and Jeffords thought the Other Side might be planning some kind of dirty trick, and wondered if I had any talents that could help them." (Another use of the rule that you should always tell the truth, with codicils, like the one upcoming.) "Unfortunately, I wasn't any use to them, so I'm still looking for work. Why don't you guys hire me?"

They smirked at one another, as Jeffords at last popped into an elevator and the door slid shut behind him. Moustache said, "*Us* hire you? To do what, Mr. Meehan?"

"Break into hotel rooms for you," Meehan said. "Like, I wouldn't leave a lot of fingerprints up there, or a bribed desk clerk down here that'll fold the first time a cop frowns at him."

"Oh, come on," Moustache said.

Meehan waved the little business cards. "You could hire me, or I could put in a complaint. You broke into my room."

"You won't do that," Bowtie said.

Meehan grinned at him. "That's cause you think I'm tied up with Benjamin and Jeffords, and so I don't want to make any waves, so you were safe to bust into my room just to see if you could find anything in there to tell you what's going on. But I'm *not* tied up with anybody at all, I'm just a guy looking for a job. So maybe you could give me a job with you guys, or I could prepare my lawsuit against your paper by calling the cops."

Moustache permitted himself to look stern. "It could be to your advantage to have a friend in the press, Mr. Meehan," he said.

Meehan said, "Does anybody actually have a *friend* in the press? Aren't you guys just halfway up the ladder, kissing the ass above you and kicking the face below you?"

They stood, as one man, like a drill team. "I hope you won't be sorry," Bowtie said, "that you decided to take this attitude toward us."

"As to your calling the police," Moustache said, "I'll hold my credibility up against a convicted felon any day."

Meehan laughed; he couldn't help it. "Credibility!" he cried. "Mary wept! Credibility!"

The press departed, shoulders squared, and Meehan went up to the room to see that Jeffords had, of course, caused his message light to start blinking. He deleted without listening; let the jerk stew until morning.

# 40

"I DIDN'T KNOW what to think," Jeffords said.

"Sure you did," Meehan said. "You thought I was selling you out to some reporters."

"You all looked so cosy together there," Jeffords explained.

"You're right," Meehan said. "What I should of done, I should of stood up and shouted, 'Don't worry, Mr. Jeffords, I'm not saying a thing about you.'"

"No, no, you were right." Jeffords ate scrambled egg, and toyed with his coffee cup. "I just wish you'd called me last night."

"I was sleepy," Meehan told him, and ate a piece of bacon.

It was six-fifty in the morning, and they were in the Crowne Royale's coffee shop, along with a few solitary salesmen and army recruits. "I barely slept at all," Jeffords said, "not knowing."

"You can sleep on the drive," Meehan told him, looking across the coffee shop and out its front window. "I think that's our car."

Jeffords turned, crouched, craned to see. "He's early."

"Good, let's get out of here."

Their waiter was a young Hispanic suffering from expression deficit disorder. Jeffords waved at him, doing the signing-in-air gesture that means bring-my-bill, and he brought it. Since he looked mostly like his own death mask, but with its eyes open, he was hard to face directly. Fortunately, he immediately went away again, and Jeffords pushed the bill toward Meehan, saying, "I checked out, so you'll have to put it on your room."

Meehan added a tithe and a signature and his room number and said, "You're getting your wallet, you can give it to me in cash. Fourteen bucks."

"Prices in New York," Jeffords said.

When they went outside, the man taking his chauffeur's cap off at the wheel of the limo was, surprisingly enough, Bruce Benjamin. Rolling his window down, he said, "Hello, you chaps. I suppose one of you wants to drive. I find it looks better if one wears the cap."

"I'll drive," Meehan said.

Climbing out of the limo, Benjamin said, "Pat and I'll ride in back."

Meehan said, "Since when are you coming along?"

"Just for a little chat," Benjamin assured him. "You can drop me off anywhere."

Jeffords was already sliding into the back seat, but Meehan said to Benjamin, "Chat about what?"

"Well, first, what you and Ms. Goldfarb did for Pat yesterday was amazing. Well above and beyond. My congratulations to you both."

Uncomfortable, Meehan shrugged and said, "We're used to having him around."

"Then," Benjamin said, "when Pat called me last night . . ."

"I get it. Climb aboard."

They all boarded, and Meehan put on the cap, which fit pretty well. He adjusted the mirror so he could see the two back there, Benjamin giving Jeffords his wallet and watch. "Don't forget my fourteen bucks," Meehan said.

"I won't."

Meehan put the car in gear, drove to the first red light, stopped, and said, "You want to know what happened last night."

"Yes, please," Benjamin said.

"I'll tell you," Meehan said, and started them forward as the light turned green. "But then, you know, I've been thinking about it, and I'm glad you're here, because I got some questions of my own, and it would be tougher to get answers just from Jeffords."

Benjamin said, "But do clear up last night for me first, please."

"I was out to dinner—"

"With Elaine Goldfarb," Jeffords interjected.

Even at this distance, in the little mirror, by dawn's early light, Meehan could see Benjamin's eyebrows raise, as he murmured, "Oh?"

Meehan took the right at the next corner and headed for the West Side Highway. "When I got home—alone—those two bozos were in my room. So I left them there and went down to the lobby—"

"Excuse me," Benjamin said. "You *left* them there? In your room?"

"There's two of them," Meehan said, "they're already in there, I got nothing in there they can't look at, or even take away with them, and I'm not in a mood for conversation, so I left."

"Unorthodox," Benjamin commented, "but I've remarked that in you before."

"Well," Meehan said, "by the time they followed me down to the lobby, I'd figured out they were reporters. I was just about to tell them to take a hike when Jeffords walked in. I knew Jeffords didn't want them to see him, so I kept talking to the guys until he finally cleared out."

"I had to *wait* for the elevator," Jeffords pointed out.

"After you got done staring at *me* for half an hour," Meehan told him. "Anyway, they got something, but they don't know what it is. They know I already met with you two, so there's some more of that famous security of yours. They said they were following up on a rumor that you guys were planning an October Surprise for the Other Side, and you got me out of a federal penitentiary, which is two wrong for two, but still, it means they know there's *something* out there. They're in the ballpark. They're not in the game yet, but they are in the ball-park."

"I know those two," Benjamin said, not sounding happy about it. "They may have the wrong end of the stick at this point, but they do have hold of the stick, and they know they have it, and they're not likely to give up."

Jeffords said, "Bruce, by this afternoon it won't matter. And I really don't believe they'll get the entire situation doped out before then."

"And they're not trailing us right now," Meehan said, with another look at his outside mirror.

Benjamin accepted that, but Jeffords said, "What?" and twisted around to look out back.

Benjamin said, gently, "Pat, he says they're *not* behind us."

"Well, I hope not," Jeffords said, facing front again, shooting his cuffs.

One final red light turned green, and Meehan steered the limo onto the West Side Highway. He'd driven trucks bigger than this, but never anything exactly *like* this; a car, but far too long. It was like driving a tunnel. The outside mirrors, left and right, showed him the world, but the inside mirror showed him the tunnel. Looking in it, he said, "Can I ask my question now?"

"Of course," Benjamin said.

"Those reporters aren't gonna work things out today," Meehan said, "but sooner or later they'll figure it out, and they'll figure out what my job was. Which means I gotta know, after all, what I'm doing here."

They were both surprised back there. Benjamin said, "But you *do* know, Francis, you've known all along."

"I'm going to get the package," Meehan said, "and I'm gonna turn it over to you."

"That's right," Benjamin said.

"The package," Meehan said, "is a videotaped confession and some documents, you told me that down in North Carolina."

"Exactly," Benjamin said.

"Everything's been fine up till now," Meehan said, "but now there's press in it, that means publicity—"

"We certainly hope not," Benjamin said.

"I don't trust hope," Meehan told him. "So maybe I'll do this thing for you, and maybe I won't—"

"We have a deal!" Jeffords cried.

"Sue me," Meehan suggested. "I'm in a different position now from when you got me out of the MCC—"

"We," Benjamin pointed out, "are the reason for that different position."

"I know that," Meehan said. "You're great guys, I wouldn't be drivin this limo without you. But does this confession and these documents mean even *more* trouble, so after I go get them and give them to you am I gonna find myself stuck in whatever's *worse* then the MCC?"

"Of course not, Francis," Benjamin said.

"I'm glad to hear you say that," Meehan said, "but I'd like to hear more."

"For God's sake, Francis," Jeffords cried, "don't you *trust* us?"

Meehan let that sentence bounce around the tunnel back

there awhile, and then he said, "Mr. Benjamin, you're closer to him than I am, would *you* answer that?"

"I believe the question was rhetorical," Benjamin said.

"Declarative," Jeffords suggested.

"Perhaps even idiotic," Benjamin said. "But I do take your point, Francis, and I believe you're right. I was hoping it wouldn't come to this, but it has."

"You're gonna tell me what's in the package," Meehan said.

Benjamin's sigh could be heard way up here at the front of the tunnel. "I'm afraid I am," he said.

# 41

"If you don't mind," Benjamin began, "I'd like to pave the way, give you a little background here."

"Sure."

"What we're talking about is the Middle East." Benjamin paused, leaned forward a little, and said, "You have heard of the Middle East."

"Sure," Meehan said, doubtfully. Most of the traffic was southbound, coming into the city, so Meehan had the northbound lanes mostly to himself.

"Well, what we have in the Middle East," Benjamin went on, "is a group of little countries that really ought to be one big bloc, but they aren't. One religion, one language, one common enemy, but it isn't enough. They don't like one another, they don't trust one another, they're like a dysfunctional family."

"They *are* a dysfunctional family," Jeffords said.

"That, too," Benjamin said. "Also, some of them are rich, with oil, and some of them are poor."

"With sand," Jeffords said.

"So, geopolitically," Benjamin said, "what we do is, we deal with them as best we can."

Meehan said, "Because you want their oil, I know that much."

"Naturally," Benjamin said. "If they didn't have oil, they could go lose themselves, like the Guatemalans. But they *do* have oil—"

"Some of them," Jeffords said.

"And some of the ones that do," Benjamin continued, "are sometimes in alliances with some of the ones that don't, and sometimes not."

Steering around a slow-moving sightseer, Meehan said, "Is this gonna go on long?"

"The point is," Benjamin said, speaking more rapidly, "for stability in the region, and sometimes for a friendly vote at the UN, sometimes we help one of them here, sometimes we help another one there. Now to the specifics."

"Okay," Meehan said. The limo had an E-Z Pass box on the windshield, up behind the mirror, so he only had to pause at the tollbooths.

"In this region," Benjamin said, as the tollbooths slid by, "there are two countries, neighbors, who don't get along very well. I'd rather not mention any names here."

"Fine with me," Meehan said.

"But neither of them is Egypt or Israel," Jeffords said, "so it's nothing to do with those guys."

"Though they'd love to know about this, God knows," Benjamin said.

"And we'd hate it," Jeffords said.

"Yes. In any event, of these other two countries, the one with the oil is usually not a friend of ours—"

"Uppity pricks," Jeffords said.

"And the one without the oil," Benjamin went on, "usually *is* a friend of ours."

"Needy pricks," Jeffords said.

"But there came a time, not long ago," Benjamin said,

"when we needed a favor from the unfriendly one. What we offered they didn't want, and it was a moment, the other country at that time was being just a little too neutral, getting up our nose, so POTUS finally said, the hell with it, show them the SLAR."

Meehan said, "Wait a minute. I remember POTUS. What's the other one, secretary of labor?"

"No, no," Benjamin said. "SLAR is Side Looking Aerial Reconnaissance, it's airborne radar, it bounces at a slant off the earth, it shows amazing details."

Jeffords said, "You can find sunken vessels, lost mines, underground streams."

"Pretty good," Meehan said.

"Well, what we had," Benjamin said, "from the SLAR, that neither of those countries knew about, was another little lake of oil. It was deeper than the other deposits around there, neither of them had discovered it yet, and we'd known about it for three or four years, keeping it as a hole card, use it when it's useful."

Meehan said, "A lake of oil. Where?"

Benjamin said, "Under both countries."

Jeffords said, "Whichever one finds out about it, sucks it all up."

Meehan said, "So your president said, give it to the rich guys?"

"At that moment," Benjamin said, "we needed the rich guys."

Jeffords said, "And the poor guys were being just a little too neutral, if they're going to be that poor."

Benjamin said, "And we'd run out of other beads to give those people."

"Okay," Meehan said, "so POTUS said, give 'em the SLAR, and they did. Then what?"

"Unfortunately," Benjamin said, "what they got showed them a little more than we wanted to show them."

"Unavoidable," Jeffords said.

"That, too," Benjamin agreed. "We simply couldn't show them what they needed to see to get at that little lake unless we showed them some other details as well."

"Hidden recon posts," Jeffords said. "Ours, and other people's."

"Refugee camps."

"Training bases."

Meehan said, "So what happened?"

"Bloodshed," Jeffords said.

Benjamin said, "Well, that's what happens in that part of the world anyway, but unfortunately—"

"Unavoidably," Jeffords said.

"That, too," Benjamin said. "But there we are, you see. The thing has POTUS's fingerprints all over it."

Meehan said, "So what?"

Benjamin wasn't comfortable about this part; he was squirming a bit, down at his end of the tunnel. "Well, you know," he said, "without meaning to, without let's say thinking it through, in the heat of the moment—"

"Pressure of the office," Jeffords said.

"That, too," Benjamin agreed. "The point is, POTUS went a bit over the line."

Meehan said, "What line?"

Benjamin said, "Well, unk-um, uh, into what I'm afraid we'd have to call a felony."

He *really* didn't want to get to the point. Meehan said, "*What* felony?"

"Well, espionage."

"*What?*"

Jeffords said, "The legal definition of espionage is the turning over of secret government information to unauthorized foreign governments or their representatives."

"The oil was authorized," Benjamin said. "The rest wasn't, and couldn't be, because of the damage that would inevitably follow, and that in fact did follow."

Meehan said, "I never heard of such a thing."

"Oh, it's happened before," Benjamin said. "Presidents do tend to forget that, even for presidents, there are lines that shouldn't be crossed."

"Nixon, for instance," Jeffords said.

"Very good point," Benjamin said. "Very similar situation. Richard Nixon, when president, gave the Shah of Iran top-secret military intelligence from our AWACS planes. Foreigner, not cleared. Same thing. Our intelligence people back in Washington had a fit when they found out."

Meehan said, "What did Nixon say about it?"

Jeffords said, "I don't think anybody ever had the nerve to mention it to him."

Meehan said, "Okay, so what makes this one different?"

"The bloodshed," Jeffords said, "including some of ours."

"Thank God it didn't rise to the level of treason," Benjamin said, "since we weren't actually at war with those people at that moment."

"They were on the terrorist nation list," Jeffords pointed out, and Benjamin sighed.

Meehan said, "We're still not getting to this package I'm supposed to pick up."

"Very soon now," Benjamin promised. "At the time all this happened, there were perhaps four people in the administration who knew about it. Unfortunately, and not unavoidably, one of the four happened to be a fellow with an overdeveloped conscience."

Jeffords said, "I believe his son was one of those taken out in the airfield raid."

Benjamin said, "Very well, that's mitigating. And probably what gave him the heart attack. Which, unfortunately—"

"And avoidably," Jeffords said, "if we'd only known."

"Well, unfortunately, in any case," Benjamin said, "the heart attack was not immediately fatal."

"He talked," Meehan said.

"Deathbed confession," Benjamin said. "Videotaped by his lawyer, with his wife and his priest present."

"All three of whom," Jeffords added, "are sworn to silence by their relationship with him."

Benjamin said, "And he'd made photocopies of certain documents to back up his story."

"Which he turned over to the wife, before he departed this vale."

Meehan said, "And that's the package. How'd it wind up with Burnstone?"

"The widow had it," Benjamin said, "but I'm afraid she remarried eight months later."

"The marriage didn't last," Jeffords said.

"Well," Benjamin said, "it was rather on the rebound."

Jeffords said, "It lasted long enough for lover boy to learn about the evidence and steal it when the marriage went sour."

Benjamin said, "And sell it to the Other Side."

Jeffords said, "He offered it to us first, goddamit."

Benjamin said, "But he offered it to people who didn't know a thing about it and assumed it was a fraud, and turned him down."

Jeffords said, "By the time the word got to the right people, it was too late. Lover boy had made his deal and moved to Virgin Gorda, British West Indies."

"We managed to find him there," Benjamin said, with some satisfaction, "and persuade him to tell us who he sold it to, and then learn where it was being kept."

"Huh," Meehan said. They were well out of the city now,

sailing northward through greenery. "Whoever has that package," Meehan said, "has the president's balls right in his hand."

Sharply, Jeffords said, "Don't you get any ideas, Francis."

"Not me," Meehan said.

# 42

They dropped Benjamin at the railroad station at Katonah—"Luck, chaps," was his final sally—and then continued on up interstate 684, Jeffords staying in back because it looked better that way, in a limo, Meehan giving him a quick rundown on the caper, so he'd know the players and the game. Jeffords listened, and then he fell asleep.

It was pleasant driving this tunnel by himself, through the morning, most of the traffic still coming the other way, little to distract him even after he switched to the state highway, route 22, two lanes, running northward through the Harlem Valley. It gave him time to think about what they were going to do today and how they might do it, and the changes they were going to have to make because of the limo in the job being this particular limo, with links back to Jeffords.

Meehan had noticed over the years that crooks in stories and movies always make all kinds of plans, contingencies, maps, timetables, charts, maybe even scale models of things. He'd also noticed over the years that he himself and the guys he knew never did any of that, wouldn't have the first idea how to go about it. You work up a general idea of what you

want and how you think you might want to go about it, and
then when you get there you improvise, based on the situation,
which is never exactly, precisely what you thought the situation was going to be.

That's the way it had always worked with him and the guys
he'd met along the way, though he could see sometimes that
those careful plans had a lot to be said for them. Like as though
you were building a house, you'd certainly want that plan, but
in fact they never were building a house. Robbing a house is
a different kind of thing.

Also, people who make plans in their lives and people who
make robberies are two pretty distinct character types. People
who make plans are likely to make plans that eliminate the necessity of having to make a robbery in the first place. So Meehan and company, not being planners, would just get a general
idea, knock back a little bourbon right before the job to calm
the nerves, and invent to suit once the job got under way.

This time, for instance, he had to figure out something to
do with this limo. The original idea had been for Bob Clarence
to drive the limo to Burnstone, pick up the household, drive
them an hour east across Massachusetts, say he needed gas,
stop at a gas station, get out of the limo, walk around to the
back of the gas station where his personal car had already
been stashed, get in it, and drive home, to meet up with the
others tomorrow. Burnstone and party would sit in the limo
until hell froze over, or until it occurred to them the chauffeur
wasn't coming back, whichever came first.

This was the idea that Bob Clarence had found a little mean
to do to a frail old man, leave him stuck with nothing but ser-
vants in the boonies in the middle of Massachusetts, but it was
also the idea Meehan had assured Clarence he would fall in
with gladly once he'd had some full-frontal exposure to the
Clendon Burnstone IV personality.

However, this was the idea that wasn't any good any more,

because, in going for the simplest answer to any problem, Meehan had leaped on the idea of getting a campaign limo from Jeffords. But, since that limo could be easily traced back to the campaign, and probably even to Jeffords, it could no longer be abandoned. So at this point, the idea had a little glitch in it, because there would come a moment when Bob Clarence was driving hither and yon around Massachusetts, but would want to sever his relationship with the Burnstone household, and what then?

Meehan didn't think Clarence would want to just shoot them all, though by that time he might very well be ready to shoot IV. Still, he might have found himself with warm, or at least civil, feelings toward the staff. And in any case, getting bloodstains out of a limo was not an easy thing to do.

And beyond all that, bloodshed was not a part of Meehan's MO, nor the people he hung out with, though the occasional tap with a sap might be called upon, or a bit of tying up. So what it came down to, the job had started, and he still had parts of it to figure out. Not the first time this had happened, but it always tended to make him nervous, which was why the bourbon, but which he didn't intend to dip into until he'd met up with the others and was no longer driving this tunnel.

Nine-thirty was the time for the meet in the fairgrounds parking lot south of Sheffield, and nine-forty was when Meehan steered off route 7, seeing the tall-sided black delivery truck tucked unobtrusively over by the weed-overgrown chain-link fence. There were no fairs on display on this Wednesday in mid-October, so they had the weedy parking area to themselves.

Bernie and Bob climbed down from the truck as the limo jounced toward them, nosing across the potholed gravel like an anteater looking for lunch, the agitation bouncing Jeffords

up out of sleep, to stare open-eyed around at this barren landscape and say, "What? What?"

"End of the line," Meehan told him. "All transfer."

By the time they stopped next to the truck, Jeffords had
reacquainted himself with the world and his position in it. He
blinked out at Bob and Bernie, finally realized that Bob wasn't
going to open the door for him even though Bob was in his
chauffeur suit—a very nice tailored navy blue, with matching
billed cap—so he opened the door himself and staggered out
to cold midmorning sunshine, where he stood stretching and
creaking and groaning while Meehan conferred with the other
two.

Who immediately wanted to know who the hitchhiker was.
"Part of the other element in the job," Meehan explained. "The
political element."

Bob pulled his chauffeur bill lower. "Then why's he here?"

"I'll let him tell you." Turning to Jeffords, who was beginning to take an interest in his surroundings, calling him "Pat"
for the first time in his life, Meehan said, "Pat, we're all first-
name here, that's Bob and Bernie, this is Pat."

Everybody said hello, warily, and Meehan said, "Tell them
the particular screwups that brought you here."

"Unfortunately," Jeffords told them, "and avoidably, I might
add, we had some security leaks at the CC, for which I must
say I have to accept partial—"

Bob, backing toward the limo, trying to scan the entire
horizon at once, said, "You bringing cops here, man?"

Jeffords gave him a blank stare. "What?"

"No, Bob," Meehan said. "Nothing like that. Let him tell
you. Pat, make it a little shorter, okay?"

"In sum," Jeffords said, "there are some foreign nationals
who have learned of the existence of these documents, the
ones Francis means to collect today, with your quite welcome
assis—"

"Shorter," Meehan said.

Jeffords cleared his throat, hunched his shoulders, and said, "These foreign nationals know there's some sort of damaging information about our president, they don't know what it is, but they want it, to blackmail him, they tried to torture the information out of me, Francis rescued me, for which I thank you—"

"So we can't leave him behind," Meehan explained to the others, "or they'll grab him again. But so far they don't know much, so they'll keep looking around New York and Washington, and meanwhile we do it and we're outa here."

Bernie said, "But they're not gonna show up and horn in."

"Definitely not."

Bob said, "But we're baby-sitting."

"Yeah," Meehan said.

"I'll stay completely out of things," Jeffords promised.

"You're damn right you will," they told him, and then Meehan said to the others, "But we still do have one thing to work out."

Bernie looked alert. "What?"

"Originally," Meehan said, "Bob was gonna abandon the limo with that crowd in it."

"Unless I liked the old man," Bob said.

"No fear of that," Meehan said. "But we can't do that any more anyway, because this is a regular limo from the president's campaign committee that Pat's loaning us that we gotta give back. It was just easier that way. So we can't leave it somewhere with Burnstone inside it."

"Hell," Bob said, "we gotta steal us another limo."

Bernie said, "A little late for that."

Meehan said, "I've been trying to think, how do we separate Burnstone from the limo without making him suspicious?"

"Hell," Bob said, "I've got my car stashed just perfect,

where I was gonna leave them. Now, I gotta get my car back, *too.*"

Bernie said, "There's always these damn things at the last minute. Hold on, let me get my bottle."

While Bernie was getting his bottle from the cab of the truck, Jeffords hesitantly said, "If I could put an oar in? Francis?"

Meehan lowered a brow at him. "You want to *say* something?"

"Well, just a question, to start." Jeffords turned to Bob: "This car you have stashed, may I ask what it is?"

"Jag," Bob told him.

"A Jaguar? The little one, or the sedan?"

"It's a brand-new," Bob told him, with some asperity, "Jaguar Xj8, the V8 model, four-door, five-seater, white onyx."

"Oh, very nice," Jeffords said, while Meehan and Bernie both looked at Bob with new respect. "You see," Jeffords went on, "here's the little idea I had."

"No little ideas," Meehan told him.

Bob said, "No, wait, let's not be prejudiced just because he isn't one of us. Hear him out."

"And *then* be prejudiced," Bernie suggested. He had his bottle now, and was grinning slightly.

Meehan shook his head at Jeffords. "This better be good."

"Well, I don't know if it is or not," Jeffords said, "but there *is* a phone in the limo, I know that much."

Bob said, "There's a phone in every limo."

"Yes, of course," Jeffords said. "And *I* have my cellphone. Now, if you can get me to where your car is—"

Bob was beginning to look prejudiced. "*You* want to drive *my car?*"

"I've never had an accident in my life," Jeffords assured him. "But here's my idea. At a given point, you, in the limo, have a breakdown. You say, 'Oh, dear, I'd better phone ahead to where you're supposed to speak,' and you phone *me*. I'll give you my . . ." hushed voice ". . . cellphone number, which I never give to anyone, and which I pray you not to give to anyone else—"

"Get on with it, Pat," Meehan said.

"All right, fine. You, Bob, phone me, I come to where you are in your Jaguar, I say I was sent by the organization where this fellow Burnstone is supposed to speak, I'll take them the rest of the way. They pile in—"

Bob said, "Why don't I take over the Jaguar?"

"No no," Jeffords said, "the chauffeur stays with the limo."

"He's right about that much," Meehan said.

"Thank you," Jeffords said. "So now I take these people to some high school or town hall or something, I say, 'Oh, everybody's inside, it's because we're late, it's already started, you all hurry in while I park the car.' They get out of the car, I drive back here."

Bob said, "Why don't I do that in the limo, drop them off somewhere, leave?"

"Because the chauffeur gets out of the limo," Jeffords told him, "to open all the doors. There isn't time to get away before they discover the town hall's empty. *I'm* a busy man, other appointments, I sit impatiently at the wheel as they get out, then zip away like a bunny rabbit."

"Careful with my car," Bob said, and Bernie said, "Like a bunny rabbit?"

"In any event," Jeffords said, "that's my contribution."

They all looked at one another. Bob said to Meehan, "Whadaya think?"

"I think," Meehan said, "if it wasn't for Pat, it could work."

"Well, you know," Bob said, "I can't drive the limo *and* the Jag, so we need another driver."

Somewhere in the ten thousand rules, it said something about not accepting contributions from amateurs, but some-

where else in there it said you adapt to circumstances. Therefore, "Maybe so," Meehan finally said.

"I can be very realistic in the part," Jeffords promised him,
"because in fact I have *played* that part several hundred times
in my career, delivering the VIP to the place where the speech
is to be made. I could do it in my sleep. Particularly with that
Jaguar, I won't raise a single question in their minds."

Meehan said to Bob, "It's your Jag."

Bob said, "No, it's the goddam limo you showed up in,
with strings attached."

Bernie took a swig from his bottle. "I think it's great," he
said. "Also, it means this bird isn't just a witness, he's one of
us."

"Well, that's true," Meehan said.

Belatedly, Jeffords looked alarmed. "One of you? One of
what?"

"The criminal enterprise, it's called," Bernie told him.

Meehan smiled at Jeffords in honest pleasure. "Welcome
aboard," he said.

# 43

WHILE MEEHAN AND BERNIE put on the limo a set of Massachusetts plates that Bernie had borrowed from somewhere this morning, Bob and Jeffords went over maps spread out on the limo's hood, to be sure Jeffords would know where he was once Bob had left him at the Jag, and would be able to find Bob again once the limo had "broken down," and would be able to find the rural grange hall they'd all decided would be the best place to dump the Burnstone household, and *then* would be able to find his way back to this fairgrounds, all without getting lost, arrested, exposed, kidnapped, or infected with Lyme disease. Bob mistrusted Jeffords' sense of direction, for some reason, and kept drilling him over and over until the license plate switch was complete, the limo's original plates now wrapped in burlap on the floor of the truck bed; then Bob said, "You screw up my Jag, mess it up, get the law after it, do *anything* to it, you're not only gonna hear about it from *me*, you're gonna hear about it from everybody I know."

"Bob," Jeffords said, with dignified restraint, "this is the sort of thing I *do*. Arrive in a territory, learn the lay of the land, borrow the vehicle, deliver the speaker to the audience, collect the contributions, go to the airport. The only differences this time are, no contributions, and this isn't an airport, though at that it does look like some I've seen."

Once Bob was more or less reassured about Jeffords' competence, he got behind the wheel of the limo, Jeffords took his accustomed place on the back seat, and off they went. Meehan, having collected his bottle from the limo before it left, cut the dust in his throat and said, "We might as well drive somewhere."

"Right," Bernie said, and they climbed aboard.

This truck had been borrowed in New Jersey last night, and now also was adorned with Massachusetts plates. Both doors featured silver letters reading ZIP DELIVERY over a rending of Mercury's winged cap, without any company address, and it was apparently part of one of the many small fleets that serviced the port area over there. It was a boxy thing, tall but not deep, so you could stand up in the back but feel cramped, and it was kind of tippy on curves, at least when empty, as it was now.

The hour was not yet ten o'clock, and from here they were less than twenty minutes from Burnstone Trail, but Bob wasn't due to make the limo pickup there until eleven, so they couldn't head that way yet. On the other hand, if they just hung around in an empty fairground parking lot for an hour, in full view of route 7, they just might attract the attention of a bored cop, which they wouldn't like. So they drove north awhile, looking for a gas station.

As they went, Meehan said, "That car of Bob's surprises me."

Bernie said, "Why? Bob's got good taste."

"Most guys that work in parking garages," Meehan said, "can have all the taste they want, they're still not driving around in this year's Jag. Unless they boosted it."

Bernie laughed. "*Work* at that garage? I just found out Bob *owns* it!"

"No kidding," Meehan said, understanding now why Bob could up and walk off the job any time he wanted for some late-night Chinese. "That's pretty good. He could make a lot of cash disappear in a place like that."

"Bob knows the tax laws," Bernie said, "like a child knows his ABCs."

"Maybe he could help me with my taxes," Meehan said, "if I'm out and around next year." A strange thought; he was not usually somebody in one place long enough to fill out forms.

"Sure he could," Bernie said. "For a fee."

At ten minutes past eleven, Bernie was driving the truck south on route 7 below Sheffield when here came the limo northbound. "There it is," Meehan said.

There it was. Crowded into the front seat with Bob was the couple from the famous Grant Wood painting, minus the pitchfork but plus a lot of woes and grievances. Bob, at the wheel, gave their Zip truck such a glare of malevolent hatred from under his chauffeur cap bill that it was obvious in an instant that the Clendon Burnstone IV charm had already worked its magic.

They continued to pass one another, and in the back seat, with Miss Lampry crunched up on the far side like a walnut, on the near side reclined Burnstone himself . . . talking. From the small smile on his face, he was pleased at what he was hearing himself say.

"Wow," said Bernie, continuing to watch the limo in his driver's side mirror.

Meehan said, "They'll be lucky Bob doesn't burn the limo to the ground before they make the rendezvous."

"Oh, Bob's pretty much a professional," Bernie said, as he

made the turn onto Spring Road. "But I'd hate to work for him in the garage tonight."

Once again, in this new vehicle, they drove around the NO ACCESS sawhorse and on down to the end of Burnstone Trail. The usual three cars were in position behind the guest house, with no extra vehicles anywhere to be seen. Bernie swung the truck around in a U that didn't worry too much about lawns or plantings, and backed up to the bungalow door.

Bernie was the lock and alarm man, so Meehan sat in the truck, took another swig from his bottle, and watched nothing happen back down Burnstone Trail while Bernie prowled around the outside of the bungalow, looking for defenses. He took only five minutes, and then he came around to Meehan's side of the truck and said, "Okay, come on."

Climbing down to the ground, leaving the bottle behind, Meehan said, "That was quick."

"We're out in the boondocks," Bernie said, "and the stuff in there isn't *that* valuable. They got tape on the doors and windows, alarm to a phone line, probably goes to some state trooper barracks somewhere. I bypassed the phone line, double-checked, there's nothing else."

Meehan walked with Bernie back along the side of the truck to the bungalow. Frowning at the front door, not yet opened, he said, "It just seems too easy."

"There's nothing else," Bernie assured him. "See that silver tape, along the edge of the glass? Way out here, that's high tech."

The ten thousand rules said, Never believe this is your lucky day. Meehan said, "You got a phone line tester?"

"Sure." He had a canvas bag of tools on the floor just inside the truck. "Not a bad idea," he admitted, opening the bag, handing Meehan the tester, a little black machine shaped like

a crab, with a dial on its back. "The line comes out in the corner over there. You should be able to reach it."

Walking toward the corner, Meehan said, "That's the only
line?"

"The only one."

Black phone line came out of the building at the corner,
about seven feet from the ground. Leaning against the building, standing on tiptoe, Meehan reached up and straddled the
crab onto the line, holding it so he could see the dial. "Okay,
open it."

Bernie hit the glass in the door with a wrench, reached
through the opening, and opened the door. The dial on the
crab didn't flutter. Bernie walked inside, and a minute later
Meehan heard another window shatter, this one in the door to
the gun room. Still the crab couldn't care less.

Nevertheless, straining, Meehan held the crab up there in
place and called, "Bust one of the cases."

*Crash;* tinkle-tinkle. Nothing from the crab.

Here and there among the ten thousand rules, there was a
positive one: When you're hot, you're hot. Meehan relaxed, returned the crab to Bernie's bag, and went into the bungalow
to the sweet sound of more shattering glass.

# 44

THE PACKAGE WASN'T there. They'd done everything right, and yet the package wasn't there.

To protect all these ancient firearms, they'd first spread on the truck floor Indian blankets from the bungalow's living room, then distributed a layer of rifles and muskets on top, then more Indian blankets, and so on. When they ran out of Indian blankets they used curtains from the windows and towels from the bathroom. When they ran out of guns to steal they looked at one another, and Bernie said, "So where is it?"

"In here some place."

Bernie gestured at the gun room, with its smashed cabinets, shards of glass and chunks of wood all over the floor, upended drawers, a couple of empty bottles that used to contain Burnstone's bourbon and now didn't even contain the drinkers' fingerprints. "Where?" he asked.

"Somewhere in *here*."

Feeling increasing frustration bordering on panic, mixed with a certain amount of worry about time, Meehan kicked and picked his way around the wrecked room, and the goddam package just kept on refusing to be there. It wasn't until he cut himself on a small narrow obtuse triangle of broken glass that he suddenly saw the light: "God *damn* it!" he cried, and put the bleeding finger in his mouth. Since, like Bernie, he was wearing pink kitchen rubber gloves, this didn't taste good, so he took the finger out of his mouth again.

"Don't leave that glass," Bernie said. "DNA."

"God damn, you're right." Finding the culprit, *carefully* picking it up, he said, "Bernie, we gotta get into the guest house."

"Why? You think it's there?"

"I know it's there. Come on."

Bernie followed him back outside, where Meehan dropped the glass onto the blacktop, breaking it some more, then ground it into powder beneath his heel, all the while Bernie was saying, "I don't know, Meehan, that's another whole proposition, they got an office in there plus living quarters, there's gonna be more than one phone line, maybe some different security for the office, and anyway, if the package isn't where it's supposed to be, what makes you think it's in there, when it could be anywhere in the world? Maybe they turned it over to CNN just last night."

"It's in the guest house," Meehan said, peeling off that glove so he could suck his finger. It wasn't a bad cut, but he didn't want to leave a lot of blood around. Or even a little.

Bernie grabbed his tool bag, sighed, and said, "Well, let's take a look."

Time. How long could Jeffords stall before dumping Burnstone? How long after that before Burnstone—or more likely Miss Lampry—realized the whole exercise had been faked up for the sole purpose of getting them away from this property? How long after that until they were on the phone with the state police, and how long after that until this lovely bucolic landscape filled up with sirens and red flashing lights?

As Bernie had predicted, there was more than one phone

line into the guest house. There were, in fact, three lines, which were probably for phone, fax, and computer, and maybe Burnstone and Company had gone all modern, even though they were way out here in the boonies, and maybe they had burglar-alarmed themselves through the computer, which would be impossible to tell until you'd already tripped it.

"Okay," Bernie said at last, while Meehan tried not to think about his own bottle in the truck and how time was fleeting by, "here's the best I can do."

"Good. Let's do it."

But Bernie needed to describe it first. "I can get all these phone lines busy talking to each other," he said. "*Then* I can unplug the computer right away, once we're in. But even so, I would say, get in and get out fast."

"I intend to," Meehan assured him, and jittered for another three minutes while Bernie did everything he'd said he was going to do, ending by taking his wrench to the window in the guest house's front door. Then he reached through, opened the door, looked back at Meehan, and said, "So far, so good."

"Upstairs, I need upstairs," Meehan said, rushing into the house, seeing the staircase, pounding up to the second floor as Bernie went off to off the computer.

All the rooms up here opened from a central hall. Meehan spun in a circle, found Burnstone's room—red-white-and-blue bedspread, framed antique battle flags mounted on the walls—rushed in there, and went straight to the television set on the dresser facing the bed. Atop the TV was a VCR, and atop the VCR a padded manila mailer envelope, and atop the envelope an empty videotape box with no label on it.

As Bernie, following, came into the room, Meehan was glaring at the VCR, muttering, "Every goddam one of these things is different. Here." *Power;* thumb it; green light; okay.

*Eject;* thumb it, grunchgrunchgrunch said the machine, and stuck a tape out at him.

As Meehan stuffed tape into box and box into mailer next to the folded-over sheaf of papers already in there, Bernie said, "He's been watching it?"

"Sure," Meehan said, and pawed among the other tapes stacked in their boxes beside the television set. "Deathbed confession, great video entertainment, better than *101 Dalmatians.*" He chose a tape, headed for the stairs. "I need the office, and then we're outa here."

# 45

THEY GOT TO the fairgrounds parking lot first, and Meehan said, "I could wish we'd picked a little more secluded meeting place."

"Nah, we're fine, it won't be long," Bernie told him, and here came the limo.

Bob came boiling out from behind the wheel with his chauffeur cap still on, ran to where Meehan and Bernie stood beside the truck, waved his arms like a maniac, and cried, "I'm gonna go there, burn the house down! Where's my goddam Jag, I wanna go there *now!*"

"You don't want to do that, Bob," Bernie said.

Bob yelled, "I never wanted to do nothing more— more— more *more* in my entire life!"

Meehan said, "No, Bob, what Bernie meant was, you don't wanna fill up our getaway route with fire engines."

That caught Bob's attention. "Shit," he said. "Still gotta get home, you're right."

Bernie extended what was left of his bottle. "Have a drink."

"Yes," Bob said, and drank deep, and said, "I could come back tomorrow."

"Or next week," Meehan said, "even better."

"I wouldn't want that sonofabitch to die before I got here," Bob said.

"You've seen him," Meehan said.

"I have."

"He's healthy as a moose, he'll live forever."

"We'll see about that," Bob said darkly.

Bernie said, "You know, I should take off now, you two can wait in the limo."

Meehan said, "You going direct to Leroy at Cargo?"

"Sure," Bernie said. "Then get rid of the truck."

"Tell Leroy, Bob and me'll call him soon, get an update."

"Right."

"Let me get my stuff," Meehan said, and got his stuff from the truck; the package, a big white envelope from the Burnstone office with a Betsy Ross flag next to the Burnstone Trail return address, the original limo license plates, and his bottle, now half empty; or possibly half full.

Bernie climbed back up into the truck, waved, and drove away from there. They watched him go, and then Meehan said, "We should switch these plates."

"Done."

They walked over to the limo, Meehan put the rest of his stuff on the back seat, and then they reswitched the license plates, Meehan doing the one on the back while Bob was doing the one on the front. Both finished, they met in the roomy back seat of the limo, shared a little more bourbon, and Bob said, "I read somewheres once, revenge is a dish best served cold. I'll be good and cold when I get back up here."

Meehan knew the ten thousand rules disagreed with that idea, that the ten thousand rules said, If you don't strike when you're hot, you'll forget about it. But everybody has their own belief systems, and he wasn't about to get into a theological discussion with Bob, so he merely said, "Good," and then said, "You know, Bob, if you're willing, you could do me a favor."

Bob gave him a Judge T. Joyce Foote fish-eye. "I ain't known you *that* long," he said.

"It's not that deep a favor," Meehan said.

Bob nodded, reserving judgment. "I'll listen," he agreed.

"In that garage of yours," Meehan said, "I bet you got some places you could stash stuff, nobody'd *ever* find it."

"Well, sure," Bob said. "That's my home base."

Meehan picked up the white Burnstone Trail envelope and showed it to Bob. "You take this," he said. "When Jeffords gets here, tuck it away somewhere he won't notice, under your coat or whatever, and when you get to that garage of yours tuck it where *nobody's* gonna notice it."

Bob took the envelope and considered it. He raised an eyebrow at Meehan and then at the envelope. "For how long?"

"Maybe a couple hours, maybe forever."

Bob shook the envelope, but it didn't do anything interesting. "Is this thing gonna blow up?"

"Not in your garage."

Bob thought about that. "But somewhere, it might," he said.

"We never know," Meehan told him, quoting from another important section of the ten thousand rules, "what tomorrow may bring."

# 46

IT WAS NEARLY an hour before Jeffords showed up in the Jag, and by then Meehan and Bob had grown more than ready to part company for a while. They didn't really know each other, they didn't have a lot in common, there weren't many topics they could chat about together, and the bourbon bottle was empty.

"It would help," Meehan said at one point, "if one of us was the kind of guy told all kinds of amusing and whimsical anecdotes about his past history, and capers, and marriages, and all that."

"I hate those kinds of people," Bob said.

"So do I," Meehan agreed, "but we could use one right now."

"What I could use is my Jag," Bob said. "I keep seeing it in a ditch somewhere, totaled, fucked over, and Jeffords not even scratched."

"The Jeffords not being scratched part I can buy," Meehan said.

But then, at long last, here came the silver beauty, growling in contentment, gliding like a cloud over the rough gravel parking lot. When Jeffords climbed out of the car, he had the slightly zonked look of somebody who's just had a really long and satisfying massage. He kept looking at the Jag, there beside him, and patting it with his fingertips.

Meehan and Bob got out of the limo to come over to the Jag, Bob immediately making a slow and suspicious circuit of the entire car, squinting, stooping, looking for the slightest scratch, while Meehan said, "That took a long time."

"Well, I was supposed to keep them away while you did your work," Jeffords reminded him.

"A *long* time," Meehan said.

"Well, also, I have to admit," Jeffords said, "I did do a bit more of a roundabout route. I just found that fellow fascinating to listen to."

Bob stopped his inspection to glare at Jeffords. "You did *what?*"

"To watch a mind like that at work," Jeffords said, and shook his head in admiration. "He processes the same information from the world that you and I do, and turns it into something from another universe. It's like listening to somebody from the Flat Earth Society, or those people who believe the moon landings were faked on soundstages in Hollywood."

Meehan said, "It almost sounds as though you admire the guy."

"I admire the effect," Jeffords said. "If *I* could tap into the subtext of fears and prejudices and prides and misunderstood history the way he can, only with a little more self-awareness, bring it out a little smoother, a little blander, I wouldn't be a groundling in the CC, I'd be running for president myself."

"You won't get my vote," Bob said, and said to Meehan, "Goodbye."

"Goodbye," Meehan agreed.

Bob got into his Jag and roared off. Jeffords and Meehan

walked over to the limo as Jeffords said, "I take it your expe-
dition was a success."

"Oh, yeah."

"You got the, um, incriminating material?"

Meehan pointed at the package in the limo, on the front
passenger seat. "He kept it in his bedroom, to watch the tape."

"Did he?" Jeffords laughed. "Well, wouldn't *you* be
tempted?"

"Watch somebody in a bed, dying? I don't think so."

"Well, give me the package, and let's be off."

Meehan opened the rear door. "Climb aboard," he said. "I'll
give you the package when we get to the city."

Jeffords grinned at him. "Francis? Don't you trust me?"

"Sure I do," Meehan said. "I just wanna round it off with a
happy ending."

"I love happy endings," Jeffords said, and got into the limo.

They headed south, Meehan wearing the chauffeur's cap—
not Bob's nice navy blue one, but the brown one that came
with this car—while Jeffords at the other end of the tunnel
played with his cellphone, having the occasional murmured
conversation, or leaving a message; all CC stuff, from what
Meehan could hear, the logistics of a presidential campaign,
the day job Jeffords had been skimping on recently.

At one point, with Jeffords off the phone for a second, Meehan called to him, "Give Goldfarb a ring, will you?"

"Sure. What am I saying to her?"

"We'll all meet at her place," Meehan said. "That's where I'll
give you the package."

"Fine. You know," Jeffords said, "we're gonna need to eat
lunch along the way."

The limo's dashboard read 1:17. "Sure. Tell her we'll get
there late afternoon."

"There's a diner in Hillsdale, New York," Jeffords suggested. "That isn't really out of our way."

"Fine."

Jeffords played with his phone some more, then said, "She wasn't in, I left a message."

Back at *her* day job, no doubt, at the MCC. "Wow," Meehan said.

Jeffords, down there at his end of the tunnel, looked interested. "Wow?"

"I was just thinking about the MCC," Meehan told him.

Jeffords' face wrinkled up. "For God's sake, why?"

"That's probably where Goldfarb is."

"Oh."

"I'm just out a week today," Meehan said. "Wednesday to Wednesday. What a week."

"For all of us, Francis," Jeffords said.

At the diner in Hillsdale, they sat in a booth in the no-smoking section, by a window with a view out over route 22, and Jeffords told the blonde waitress he wanted pastrami on rye. Meehan said, "I'll have the cheeseburger and the side of onion rings and a side of pickles." When asked, they both admitted to a desire for coffee.

She went away, and Meehan looked out at the limo and the gas station/convenience store across the way and wondered what his future was going to be, now that he was going to have one. Then their food was brought and they both dug in. Meehan had his chauffeur cap and the package on the bench seat beside him, by the wall, but he had to pick both up and put them on his lap when the two Busters joined them, one sliding in beside Meehan, one beside Jeffords.

Meehan, the burger turning to demolition debris in his mouth, said, "Oh, Jeffords."

Jeffords had the grace not to look Meehan in the eye. "Believe it or not, Francis," he said, "I am sorry about this."

"*You're* sorry!"

"I am. I'll have some troubled times, remembering all this."

"I *rescued* you!" Meehan reminded him. "I saved your life. At the very least, I saved your fingers."

"I know that," Jeffords acknowledged, nodding, tapping those fingers on the Formica table. "That doesn't make it easier."

"But why do it at *all?*"

Now Jeffords did look Meehan in the eye, and nothing Meehan saw there helped him. Jeffords wasn't vicious, or vindictive, or angry, or evil, or any of that. He was just a low-level clerk, doing a job. He said, "Francis, you can't be left out in the world."

"Why not?"

"You're an anomaly, you're an entire bushel basket of questions just waiting to be asked. You're a forty-two-year-old man on probation at juvenile court. You're a recidivist felon, supposed to be in a federal penitentiary, out of the MCC with absolutely no good reason, no paperwork that would hold up to any serious scrutiny. And now let's say, just for argument, let's say, somewhere down the line, you get mad at us, or depressed, or drunk, or want to hold us up for money, or for whatever reason, you start to talk."

"I've never talked," Meehan said.

"There's always a first time," Jeffords said, and Meehan hated it when people quoted the ten thousand rules back at him. "What it comes down to," Jeffords said, and now he seemed almost embarrassed, "and I hate to say this, it's such a cliche from old movies and mystery stories, but the fact is, Francis, you know too much."

Grimly aware that argument would get him nowhere, but having to try it because you have to try everything, Meehan said, "Whadaya mean, I know too much? You talking about *killing* me?"

"No, of course not," Jeffords said. He sounded both appalled and insulted. "What do you take us for?"

"Then I'm *still* gonna know too much."

"The whole purpose here," Jeffords explained, being kind to him, "is merely to remove your credibility. If you were to decide to go public, and here you are on the loose when you shouldn't be, swathed in all these legal anomalies, people would listen to you, they'd be intrigued by you, they'd follow up and they'd find *us*. But if you're just one more disgruntled con, writing crazy letters from your prison cell, making wild accusations about respectable citizens, no one will give you the time of day. You see, Francis? It's the only thing we can do."

Meehan saw. That was the worst of it, sometimes, being able to see the other guy's point of view. "I didn't think you'd do this to me, Jeffords."

Jeffords sighed. "Oh, they never do," he said. "It gets them all, though, sooner or later. They've been warned, they know better, they know all the bitter histories, but they just can't help themselves. They *want* to believe. Everybody, somewhere down the line, trusts a politician."

# 47

"Not quite everybody," Meehan said.

He picked the package out of his lap, off the chauffeur cap, and placed it on the table beside the cheeseburger he'd never eat. With the tip of one finger, he slid it across the Formica toward Jeffords, who watched it coming with sudden mistrust. He looked at Meehan's face, and what he saw there he didn't like. He said, "What have you done, Francis?"

"You never for a second meant me to stay out of the MCC," Meehan told him. "I could smell it on you, you and Benjamin, slumming a little because you needed an expert, an outsource. And you were doing me a favor, look at it that way, giving the little felon an extra bonus vacation out in the world before he gets to be locked away forever in—whadaya call it? A facility. Facile for you to say."

Up till now, the Busters had merely been sitting there, two new ones very like the previous ones, but now they could both be seen to take an interest in that package, and the one beside Jeffords said, "Mr. Jeffords, you think it's rigged? You want me to take it outside and open it?"

"No no," said Jeffords, and sighed. "That isn't going to be

the trouble." He looked bleakly at Meehan. "You won't tell me, will you? I have to open it."

"Why should I spoil the surprise?"

Jeffords sighed again. He hefted the package. "A tape, and some papers."

"Very good," Meehan told him.

Jeffords squeezed open the end of the package and looked inside. "A tape, and some papers."

"Still the same."

"Not the same, though," Jeffords said. "No, I doubt that. Not at all the same."

He tilted the package, and out came the folded sheets of Burnstone Trail letterhead stationery and the videotape in its brightly colored box. Turning the tape box with one finger, like a laboratory sample, he spoke the words of the title: "The Green Berets."

"John Wayne," Meehan told him. "Wayne directed it, too. Produced by his son Michael. Talk about your deathbed confession."

"You gave it to one of your friends," Jeffords said.

Meehan lifted an eyebrow at him. "Friends? Who would that be?"

"Those two you did the, the thing with," Jeffords said, waving vaguely and irritably at route 22 outside the window. "The white one, and the black one."

"They're not my friends," Meehan said. "The black one I never met before we set up this job. The white one I worked with a couple times over the years. Mr. Jeffords, in my line of work, you don't hang around with the other guys like your *friends*. Those are people, and I'm one of them, the law could show up at any second, in Kevlar. Unless you're working with those people, you stay *away* from them. You don't all live in the same neighborhood, like cops or jazz musicians, your wives in the same reading group, kids in Little League together.

You don't help out, hold things for one another. We are what we are because what we are is *solitary*."

"You did *something* with it," Jeffords insisted.

"Sure I did," Meehan said. "While you were driving around Massachusetts, fascinated, listening to one of the finest minds of the thirteenth century."

"Oh, God," Jeffords said. "I left you alone too long."

"It's up to me now," Meehan said. "If something makes me unhappy, that package is gonna show up like a summer movie. If nothing makes me unhappy, maybe nobody will ever see the thing again."

Jeffords said, "Maybe? You want more money?"

"Sure," Meehan said. "Everybody wants more money. But it isn't money's gonna keep me quiet, Mr. Jeffords. You gonna give me money, and *then* throw me back in the MCC? I don't think so."

Jeffords said, "So what *do* you want?"

"I've got it," Meehan said, and spread his hands as much as he could, being tucked in between a Buster and a wall. "My freedom."

Jeffords thought it over. Then he shrugged and offered Meehan a weak grin, and said, "Well, I can certainly tell Bruce I tried."

"I'll give you a note, if you want."

"No, that won't be necessary, he'll see the situation." Jeffords shook his head. "You see, Francis," he said, "what it comes down to, what *we* want, the people like Bruce and me and the president and all the rest of us, and that oaf Burnstone and *his* candidate, what we want is control. We wanted to end this with the evidence in our hands and you back in the MCC, and everything under control."

"But no," Meehan said.

"It disturbs us," Jeffords said, "something being out of our control. It makes us uneasy."

"In case you think," Meehan said, "that it would make you *so* uneasy that maybe you should have these fellas here take me down the road and lose me, let me just tell you, my turning up disappeared will bring out that tape." A lie, but so what?

But Jeffords was waving that away, saying, "No, don't even think about that, Francis, that's for the melodramas. It's tough enough to keep your footprints unnoticed when you're doing a simple little dirty trick on the Other Side. If we already knew we couldn't successfully pull a burglary on our own, trust me, we know better than to think we could pull off a murder."

"Get another expert."

Jeffords' laugh was bitter. "Are you kidding? Look at the trouble we've got from the first one. Besides, every professional hit man in America is actually an undercover FBI agent, as every schoolboy knows, and as is demonstrated regularly in headlines in the newspapers. No, you're free, goddamit. You gonna finish your lunch?"

"No. You made me lose my appetite."

"Sorry." To the Busters he said, "We're going now." They stood, and Jeffords said, "I'll take the check here."

"Thanks. And leave me a hundred, will you? Walking around money."

Jeffords pursed his lips. Reaching for his wallet, he said, "I should've left you in the MCC."

"Whoever else you got would've been worse."

"Christ, and that's probably true, too," Jeffords said, dropping greenbacks next to the onion rings.

"Don't forget your hat," Meehan said, extending the chauffeur's cap.

Jeffords took it. "The next time they catch you," he said, "you'll be on your own."

"No, I won't," Meehan said.

\* \* \*

The first time he tried to call, from the diner, he hung up just before the answering machine would have come on. Then he spent some of Jeffords' hundred—ninety, Jeffords had given him, actually—on a cab from the diner the twenty miles westward to the railroad station in Hudson, along the Hudson River, where he tried calling again, and again avoided the answering machine.

He had time then to sit for a while, on the platform, looking out from the station at the wide slow river and all of America beyond it, and to think that, if he cared about it, he could probably decide the upcoming presidential election right now, all by himself. But that would mean *looking* at those people, those candidates, getting involved, studying their histories and their programs, making an informed decision; so screw it. Let the Americans work it out for themselves. How bad a choice could they make?

After the third failed phone call, he sat on a bench inside the station, just waiting it out, and was there when the two guys walked in, looked around, looked at him, and then walked straight toward him. Oh, come on, he thought. Enough is enough.

The two guys were not quite twins. They were both bareheaded, with thick black hair heavily piled all over their skulls. Both had smoky skin with darker beard-shadow and rich black moustaches. Both wore dark vinyl zip-up jackets zipped up, and creased clean blue jeans, and short black boots. Both were a little bigger than necessary, and so were their noses. One of them wore aviator-style glasses, clear, and the other one didn't.

Meehan sighed and waited, and the two came over to sit on the bench, one on either side of him. The one on his right, with the aviator glasses, said, "You will stand and come outside to our car now, or we will shoot you. We don't care."

Meehan frowned, leaning toward him, listening. He said, "Would you say something?"

They gave each other surprised looks. The one with the aviator glasses said, "I already said it. Do you want to die?"

"Ah," Meehan said, working it out. "So you're Mostafa." Pointing at the other one, on his left, he said, "So that makes you Yehudi."

Yehudi shook his head. "Why do you say that?"

"Sure, that's it," Meehan said, agreeing with himself. "You're the one talked to me on the phone." Turning back to Mostafa he said, "I never saw either of you guys, but I heard you talk."

Mostafa scrinched the eyes up behind the aviator glasses. "You heard us talk?"

"Sure. I was in the closet at Goldfarb's when you showed up, with the electric tape on the door so it wouldn't lock? That jacket you're wearing, you put that in the closet, you keep some kinda pistol in that pocket there. I touched it."

They both stared at him. Mostafa said, "You touched my pistol?"

"Listen," Meehan told him, "I'm not the one you should worry about. I *left* the pistol there. I just wanted to see you two, no confrontations, but when I was going to go take a look at you in the kitchen, drinking tea there—"

"This is craziness," Yehudi said. "What are you making up here?"

"I'm the one left the ladder in the elevator," Meehan told him. "Remember? Mostafa told you there was a ladder in the elevator."

"I did," Mostafa said. He sounded awed.

"So," Meehan said, "I'm gonna go take a look at you, just a quick peek, and Goldfarb comes out of the bedroom with your handcuffs on one wrist and carrying a pistol of her own. She was gonna shoot you two, no kidding."

They looked at each other past him, frowning, and Mostafa

said, not to Meehan but to Yehudi, "It was the woman who had the pistol, at Victor's."

"Oh, Reader, you mean," Meehan said. "Yeah, that's the point I'm making. I talked her out of it at her place, killing you, with cleaning all those bloodstains off her kitchen, but *she's* the one you gotta look out for, not me. And by the way, the job's over."

Neither of them liked that. Mostafa, apparently trying to be tricky, said, "What job?"

"The job you wanted to know about," Meehan explained. "The package, some kind of evidence could make some kind of trouble for the president. I got it, I don't know what it is, I don't *wanna* know what it is, and I gave it to Jeffords just a couple hours ago, which is why I'm here, waiting for the train. But the point is, you do something to me, Goldfarb'll tear your hearts out. This is just a friendly warning."

They both remained silent, so he got to his feet, turned to look at them, and said, "And here's another question you oughta ask yourself. How long are *you* two gonna be on the same side?" He smiled goodbye, and went out to look at nothing go by on the tracks outside, and a little later, when he went back in to use the phone, they were gone.

But it was his fifth try on the phone, at quarter to six, when at last she answered: "Goldfarb."

"Meehan," he said.

"Well, hello. Where are you?"

"Not in the MCC," Meehan said, "which is where Jeffords tried to put me."

"Why, that son of a bitch. Though I'm not surprised, I must say. What, are you hiding out? Headed for Idaho?"

"No, I'm safe," Meehan said, and couldn't believe it himself. "Free and clear and safe. And I wonder if I should come back to the city and we talk."

"Meehan," she said, "I can't ask you to reform."

"No, I know."

"So I can't be around you. You understand that."

"I was thinking." he said. "I'm gonna be flush for a while, because of today."

"No details!"

"No, don't worry. But I was thinking, before I'm broke again, with your connections, you could probly set me up with one of those social services outfits, you know, counselors to ex-cons, that kind of thing."

Sounding extremely suspicious, she said, "Telling them what?"

"How to be rehabilitated," he said. "How to make the ten thousand rules work *for* you."

"The what?"

"I never told anybody about those before," he said. "That's a long conversation. Should I grab a train here, come back to the city?"